Praise for ghostgirl:

An instant *New York Times* bestseller

A *Publishers Weekly* Staff Pick

A 2008 National Parenting Publications
Gold Award Winner

A New York Public Library
"Stuff for the Teen Age" pick

A *CosmoGirl* Club pick

★ "Polished dark-and-deadpan humor, it's a natural
fit with Gen Y." —*Publishers Weekly*, starred review

★ "Fast-paced and fun yet thought-provokingly
heartwarming. Goofy, ghastly, intelligent, electrifying."
—*Kirkus Reviews*, starred review

★ "Tim Burton and Edgar Allan Poe devotees will die
for this fantastic, phantasmal read."
—*SLJ*, starred review

★ "Readers with a taste for black humor and satire will feast
on Hurley's crisp, wise dialogue. Anticipate a well-deserved
cult following." —*VOYA*, starred review

ghostgirl
Homecoming
by Tonya Hurley

Little, Brown and Company
New York   Boston

☙

Little, Brown and Company

Hachette Book Group • 237 Park Avenue, New York, NY 10017
Visit our website at www.lb-teens.com

Little, Brown and Company is a division of Hachette Book Group, Inc.
The Little, Brown name and logo are trademarks of Hachette Book Group, Inc.

First Paperback Edition: September 2010
First published in hardcover in July 2009 by Little, Brown and Company

The characters and events portrayed in this book are fictitious.
Any similarity to real persons, living or dead, is coincidental and not intended by the author.

Library of Congress Cataloging-in-Publication Data
Hurley, Tonya.
  Ghostgirl : homecoming / by Tonya Hurley.—1st ed.
  p. cm.
  Summary: When Petula becomes deathly ill, her sister Scarlet seeks help from Charlotte, for whom the afterlife has become burdensome, leaving her just as insecure and isolated as she was in life.
  ISBN 978-0-316-11359-5 (hc) / ISBN 978-0-316-08943-2 (pb)
  [1. Future life—Fiction. 2. Sisters—Fiction. 3. Coma—Fiction. 4. Death—Fiction. 5. Friendship—Fiction.] I. Title.
  PZ7.H95667Ghs 2009
  [Fic]—dc22   2008043791

10 9 8 7 6 5 4 3 2 1

RRD-C

Book design by Alison Impey

Printed in the United States of America

For Tracy, my soul.

Michael, my heart.

Isabelle Rose, my life.

ghostgirl

Chapter 1

The Slender Thread

*Answered prayers cause more tears
than those that remain unanswered.*
—Teresa de Cepeda y Ahumada

If you expect nothing, you can never be disappointed.

———◆━◆◆━◆———

Apart from a few starry-eyed poets or monks living on a mountaintop somewhere, however, we all have expectations. We not only have them, we need them. They fuel our dreams, our hopes, and our lives like some super-caffeinated energy drink. Charlotte was done living, but she wasn't done dreaming—although she definitely felt like her dreams had been put on eterna-hold.

**ying of boredom wasn't an option.**
Charlotte Usher was already dead. She
drummed her spindly fingers impassively
on her desk, then slid the three-wheeled office chair she was
sitting on to one side of her cubicle and then the other, cran-
ing her neck in hopes of getting a slightly better view down
the hallway.

"I have no life," Charlotte grumbled, just loud enough for
Pam and Prue, seated in cubicles nearby, to hear.

"Right. None of us do," Prue crowed. "Now shut it, I'm on
the phone."

"Like *you* should be," Pam chimed in, using her hand instead of the mute button to silence the receiver and keep her
"client" from hearing her talk.

As Pam and Prue chatted busily away, Charlotte stared
down resentfully at her own phone. Each phone, like the

cubicles, was identical. They were bloodred, with a single flashing light in the center. No dial pad, no way to call out. They just received.

In fact, she didn't know it was a flashing light from firsthand experience because, so far, it had never rung. It's not even as if she were down the hall and missed a call or something. It had never rung. Not once since she'd been here, which felt like a long time.

"Maybe something is wrong with the connection," Charlotte moaned, pretty much summing up not just her lack of phone time but her lack of enthusiasm as well. She spread her arms out on the desk and lay her head in them, like a pale, fragile egg in a curly nest.

"Watched nails never dry," CoCo whispered sympathetically, seeing Charlotte staring at her phone as she gamboled by her cubicle.

Sitting there day after day incommunicado was terribly frustrating and more than a little embarrassing for Charlotte. Everyone else's phone was ringing off the hook! After all, wasn't *she* the reason why all her classmates, now fellow interns, were there in the first place? Heck, even the new girl, Matilda Miner, who sat directly opposite Charlotte at work, was clucking away, fielding hundreds more calls than she was.

"I know, it sucks, right?" Maddy said, peeking her frizzy head over the divider separating them. "It sucks that no one is calling you."

Charlotte nodded halfheartedly and just as she began to spill her guts, Maddy's phone rang. Again.

"Oh, sorry," Maddy interrupted, stating what was all-too-obvious to Charlotte. "I can't talk now. I've got to get that. We can talk later, okay?"

"Sure," Charlotte said resignedly, leaning her head back down, this time twisting her eyes upward at the video camera pointed directly at her. Monitoring her? Mocking her was probably more like it.

Nevertheless, she tried to keep a stiff upper lip, like some put-upon British teenage royal in a welcoming line. If there was one thing she'd learned, it was that her conduct mattered — especially if someone was watching. She looked back down, squinting from the glare of the white walls and the incandescent office ceiling lights above and greeted her solitude with the grace and dignity befitting an intern of her pedigree. She straightened up, crossed her legs at the ankle, folded her bony fingers on her lap, pursed her lips into a tight little smile, and continued to . . . wait.

Charlotte started reflecting — something she'd been doing a lot of lately.

Choking on that gummy bear and dying in class had changed everything, but it wasn't all bad. She'd experienced a lot more personal growth in death than she ever had in her life. She learned the value of teamwork, selflessness and sacrifice through her Dead Ed classmates and of course their supportive and sympathic teacher Mr. Brain. She'd even gotten to go to Fall Ball with Damen, the guy of her dreams. Kind of, at least. Most importantly, she'd found a best friend and soul mate, Scarlet Kensington, a connection that she'd been craving her whole life. She crossed over satisfied, filled with hope

and expectation. But now, her future, which had been looking so bright there for a minute, felt more and more like a dead end. Life on the Other Side definitely wasn't what Charlotte hoped for. Instead of paradise, it was more like the day after Christmas. Every day. She started to go down a list of what was "supposed" to happen but hadn't. No pearly gates. No harps. Just more work to do.

When they'd first arrived here, she recalled, the Dead Ed kids were kept in an empty monochrome holding room, kind of like a jail cell without the bars. It was imposing and had none of the questionable charm of even the intake office at Hawthorne High. One by one, her classmates were called and led through a nondescript steel doorway. As in life, Charlotte was dead last.

"Usher," Mr. Markov, a man wearing horn-rimmed glasses and a sensible suit, had finally called. "Usher, Charlotte."

"Present!" she replied, happy that someone finally called her name, and had bothered to get it right.

"Oh, goodie," he snapped curtly, tamping down Charlotte's momentary good mood considerably. "We've been having some technical difficulty with the lines and we wanted to make sure everything was in working order so that you could start right away."

"Start? Start what?"

Charlotte was done with starts, she was ready to stop. Stop learning, working, wanting. All of that. The man didn't answer her as he led Charlotte into the other space: a room filled with uniform rectangular cubicles and phones. She stood staring for a second, at what, exactly, she had yet to determine. It

was as if the place and everyone in it was at the tail end of something that used to be alive, but was now stagnant and stuffed, almost museum-like. There was so little to notice. It was all so . . . dull.

"Does God run a home shopping channel?" she joked nervously.

She then looked around the room and some minor details began to reveal themselves. There was a desk and phone for everyone in her class, with one empty place left over. Everyone from Dead Ed was already seated, and she was glad they had made it there together, wherever "there" was.

Markov began his lecture. It was another orientation speech, but not nearly as open and interactive as Mr. Brain's was when they started Dead Ed. There was more drill sergeant than guru in this guy.

"Everything you've learned," Markov announced, "has gotten you here."

From the tone of his voice, they weren't sure if they should be proud or not.

"But here is not there. Now is not then," he said.

"What's this about?" Charlotte asked Pam quietly.

"Seems we graduated, but now we've got internships," Pam whispered from her cubicle.

"This is where you'll prove yourself, where you'll put your education into practice," Mr. Markov continued.

"This is BS," Prue snipped.

"No, it's a hotline," he said.

"A hotline? To where? For what?" Charlotte asked incredulously.

"It's for troubled teens."

"Can you be a little more specific, sir," Charlotte prodded in her most cadet-friendly tone. "In case you haven't figured it out, all teens are pretty much troubled."

Mr. Markov was an impatient sort who did not easily tolerate sarcasm from his charges, but he could see the confusion on all the interns' faces and felt obliged to elaborate.

"Have you ever had an argument with yourself?" he asked.

"All the time," Suzy Scratcher said as she reflected.

"You mean inside your own head?" Pam answered, grasping the concept ahead of the others.

"Exactly," said Mr. Markov. "You will be the voice inside someone else's head. When they are afraid or confused or lonely or perhaps contemplating something unthinkable, your phone will ring."

"Like a celebrity's sobriety coach or something?" CoCo perked up, her previous addiction to tabloids rearing its ugly head once again.

"It will be your chance to be helpful, to do good and pass along to others what you have learned," Mr. Markov added.

"It will be so cool to talk to living people again!" Charlotte shouted, seeming to miss the point a little.

"You won't actually be *talking* to them in that way, Usher," he corrected her. "You will be more like . . ."

"Their conscience," Charlotte interrupted, showing she understood better than she'd let on at first.

"Yes, that's right," Mr. Markov said.

"Be kind, rewind," Metal Mike piped in with a sample of his childish "inner voice."

Instead of disciplining Mike for his sarcastic sloganeering, Markov used his comment as an opportunity to explain further. He walked over to Mike's phone, picked it up for effect, and continued.

"Everybody needs help at one time or another," Markov said.

"Some more than others," CoCo jibed arrogantly, scanning the room.

"But," Markov continued, showing a surprisingly subtle wit, "helping is not just a *calling*, it's a skill. Something learned."

Charlotte was skeptical. Her own life experience provided plenty of evidence that sympathy, empathy for others, was either something you had or didn't. Most people didn't.

"Someone can have the best intentions," Markov said, "but offering the wrong advice, the wrong help at the wrong time, can be worse than not helping at all."

"So we are here to perfect our craft," Buzzsaw Bud interjected excitedly, the idea of becoming a skilled craftsman appealing to him greatly.

Markov nodded his approval.

"And once we do, we can leave?" Charlotte asked impertinently.

Markov raised his brow as Pam gulped and shot Charlotte a worried look.

"There's nothing keeping you here," Markov said tersely, the disapproval in his voice obvious to the whole class. "It's your choice to stay or go at any time."

It may have been her choice, but then she would also

be making a choice for all those desperate callers who were sure to be reaching out to her. That's what he really meant, she thought. He was questioning her own conscience, her own sense of responsibility. Markov didn't need to say it; his cocked brow said it all. The idea of shouldering such a burden scared her.

Markov had made his point, to Charlotte and the whole class, for that matter. They had a job to do, and it was not to be taken lightly. Not one to belabor an issue, he changed the subject.

"Before we begin, there is a bit of business we need to take care of," Markov continued. "A graduation present."

A door opened and a group of people flooded the room. Charlotte was confused. Everyone's eyes lit up with the joy of recognition. Pam, speechless, got up and ran into the arms of a kind-looking man.

"Pam?" Charlotte called after her.

"This is Mr. Paroda, my second-grade music teacher. He taught me the piccolo!"

Next, Silent Violet, no longer silent, ran screaming toward an elderly lady.

"Grandma!" Violet exclaimed as she embraced the older, silver-haired woman.

"We need to talk," the woman said as she led Violet to a corner, where they huddled close and gabbed away.

After everyone filed into the room, a glorious, elegant fig-ure appeared, only this one had a pink fitted aura.

"Darling," the impeccably dressed woman said.

"Ms. Chanel, this has always been my dream," CoCo muttered, swooning, as she reached out for her idol. "I've always wanted to make something of my life, just like you did."

"How many cares one loses when one decides not to be something but to be someone," Coco Chanel said. "That's one of my favorite quotes."

"It's an awesome, brilliant quote," CoCo said. "Who said it?"

"I did, darling," Chanel replied in all her timeless fabulousness.

Everyone in the room was paired up with long-deceased relatives, mentors, and even pets. Charlotte was moved by the touching reunions, and looked around, curious to see who was there for her. She wondered about her parents, which was the first time in a long while. Would they traipse through the door, much like they should have fifteen years ago? All she was really told about them was that they had gone out on their anniversary and never made it home.

She was only two when they died, so she probably wouldn't recognize them even if they were standing right in front of her. She reverted to an old habit and started to examine everyone's noses to see if any of them resembled hers. She remembered when her classmates' moms would come to pick them up, the teacher would say, "she has your nose," so that is what Charlotte always looked for. Her whole life she wanted someone to have her nose. But looking around now, she couldn't find a match anywhere in the crowd.

"All right, settle down, everybody," Markov interrupted,

pulling out what looked like an architectural rendering of a compound. "This will help you get your bearings."

It was a simple, circular layout and included a half-moon-shaped block of what looked like attached condos along the perimeter, each one assigned with a name tag to an intern. Charlotte was too distracted to look for her own name in the group of domiciles, but she needn't have bothered, as she would learn shortly, because it wasn't there.

A distance away from the rowhouses was the office building they were in and a larger apartment complex directly across from it. Charlotte tried to gauge how far by working out the map scale, the whole "one inch equals x many feet" sort of thing keeping her mind occupied while everyone else was busy smiling. Old habits, and defense mechanisms, die hard.

"Okay, everyone with assigned living quarters can head home for the afternoon," Markov advised to cheers from the reunited interns.

Charlotte still hadn't worked the distance out exactly, but there definitely was a long way between the "living" quarters — the description of which Charlotte found somewhat ironic — and the rest of the compound. Oddly, the whole thing looked to Charlotte like one huge happy face, the condos forming a big smile and the apartment tower and office building the vacant, dilated, nondescript eyes — like hers.

"The rest of you will find a room at the dormitory across the courtyard," Markov said plainly.

What *rest of you*, Charlotte thought? There was no one else left. He meant her.

"Enjoy your time together catching up," Markov said pleasantly as he dismissed the interns. "And . . . have a nice day."

"Nice, indeed," Charlotte groaned at Markov's closing line, feeling her happy face observation had been confirmed. "And the laugh's on me."

Everyone filed out with their significant others. Long lost souls, connected once again. The only thing Charlotte seemed to be reunited with was the old feeling of being alone. Unclaimed. It was like death by a thousand paper cuts as each coupling made their way past her. She wasn't even sure whom she *wanted* to meet again on the other side. Still, she always took it for granted that there would be someone.

"We're all alone in death . . . and some of us after," she sighed, feeling sorry for herself. As the crowd departed and the office door closed, Charlotte looked up and saw someone she hadn't noticed before, another girl sitting across the room looking at her.

The girl was definitely put together from head to toe. Her dark frizzy mane pulled up high, with not a strand out of place, accented her sharp features and full lips. Her long geometric-print frock was studiously worn and faded to make it look like she didn't care, but Charlotte knew better. There was nothing casual at all about the outfit, or the girl, at first or even second glance. She seemed to be all business, except for the flirty smile she flashed in Charlotte's direction.

"Hey," the girl called out enthusiastically, before Charlotte could actually get out the words to ask what she was doing there. "I'm Matilda. You can call me Maddy."

"Nice to meet you . . . Maddy," Charlotte said, both appreciative and a touch disconcerted by Maddy's warmth. They were total strangers after all.

"I guess we're roomies," Maddy chirped cheerfully.

"Oh, ah, I'm not sure . . . I've got to talk to Pam and Prue before . . ."

"I just assumed . . ." Maddy's voice trailed off. "Since we were the only ones left . . ."

Charlotte knew that look on her face. How it felt to reach out and be, well, rejected.

"Did any of your 'friends' offer to take you along to meet their loved ones?"

"No . . . but . . ." Charlotte started in an attempt to make excuses for her friends, but stopped herself. It was obvious she was, at least for the moment, forgotten. "You know, we're all here because of me," Charlotte said, unable to resist the urge to puff herself up in front of a new girl. "All except for you, I mean."

"That's really impressive," Maddy said offhandedly. "How soon they forget, huh?"

"Yeah," Charlotte said quietly.

"Not much point in sticking around here, then. Want to go home?"

Charlotte balked for a minute, still a little dazed and slightly demoralized by it all, but then came around.

"Sounds tempting. Let's go."

Maddy smiled back invitingly as they left the office and started across the courtyard toward the enormous, circular,

sky-scraping apartment tower that would serve as their dorm for, well, however long they were stuck there.

∽

"This is . . . home?" Charlotte asked Maddy unconvincingly as she eyed the building.

It was impressive in height but impersonal, just like the phone bank. Part obelisk, part Space Needle, perfectly suited to the strange military-type compound. Timeless and Spartan. She and Maddy walked in, stopped at the front desk, and said hello to the doorman. He looked back at them impassively, handed them keys to an apartment on the seventeenth floor, and pointed them in the direction of the elevators. Small talk, apparently, was not part of his job description.

"Seventeen?" Charlotte muttered aloud. "That's random."

"You better get used to it." Maddy shrugged matter-of-factly as they walked.

There was a crowd at the elevator, so Charlotte stopped talking. They pressed "up" and waited along with a bunch of unruly kids and a really sweet young couple — high school sweethearts, maybe — for the elevator to descend. The bell sounded, doors opened, and they all got on. The elevator started "up," slowly.

"Why should I get used to it?"

"Think about it," Maddy said. "How old are you?"

"Seventeen," Charlotte answered, still a little oblivious.

"Me too. We're seventeen and . . . always will be."

Just as it began to sink in for Charlotte, the elevator stopped

at the sixth floor and a few of the kids got off. Then at the seventh and eighth, a few more exited at each level. Her heart sank as the elevator rose.

Charlotte tried to see a positive side, but couldn't. She always looked forward to getting older as the payoff for a childhood of insecurity and loneliness. Now, there was nowhere for her future self to live, no need for a future self to exist at all, in fact, even in her mind. And that girl, that future incarnation of herself, more than anyone else, was the hardest person to say good-bye to. Charlotte watched the last of the children exit on the twelfth floor, and felt a little less sorry for herself. But only a little.

The elevator doors opened to a circular hallway carpeted with a musty gray indoor/outdoor carpet. Charlotte imagined the smell of mildew, and even though she was dead, the thought of it made her itch a little. The girls made their way to their room and Maddy slowly opened the door and flicked on the light.

"What is this?" Charlotte snorted, surveying the dank accommodations.

The room was bare, industrial looking, and "issued" with cement floors and large windows, unfurnished except for a table, two folding chairs, and two beds, if you could call them that. They were bunks, actually, stainless steel bunks that were built into the wall. The plush bedding, stained-glass windows, and carved bedposts of Hawthorne Manor were just a fond memory now.

"As if anyone would ever want to steal these," Charlotte said, tugging on the immobile bunk frames with all her might.

Touching them made the circumstances much more real to her, and much more unpleasant.

"I don't know," Maddy said, a hint of optimism in her voice. "I kind of like it here. It's . . . cool."

"It's cool, all right. Like ice."

"Hey, at least we've got each other, right?" Maddy said, trying to get Charlotte to smile.

Charlotte could come to only one conclusion: whatever *this* was, it was not a stairway to heaven.

Chapter 2

Pushing in the Pin

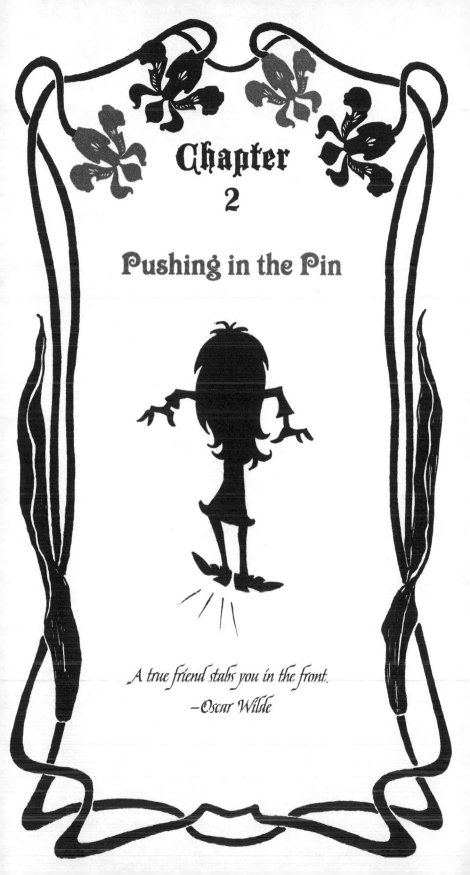

A true friend stabs you in the front.
—Oscar Wilde

How can you ever know who your friends are?

A true friend is someone who is always there for you, with no agenda other than the friendship itself. We rely on our friends to lift us up in bad times, to keep us grounded in good times, but most importantly, to be there for us when we need nothing at all. Charlotte wasn't sure who her friends were anymore, but she was sure that she needed them.

**nother day, another dolor. Charlotte** spent the evening staring out the window and then hit the sack after another uneventful day. She was quiet, making sure not to wake Maddy, who she thought had crashed after having had, yet again, a busy day at work. After a few minutes of silence, however, Maddy spoke up.

"Maybe this is none of my business, Charlotte, but . . . no, forget it."

"No, please go ahead, Maddy. We're friends. You can ask me anything."

"Do you think some of the girls at work, especially Prue and Pam, I mean, take you for granted sometimes?"

"What do you mean?"

The curiosity in Charlotte's voice suggested Maddy might

have hit a nerve. Charlotte was used to being talked to condescendingly and had pretty much let it roll off her back to the point where she didn't much notice it.

"I don't know, it just seems like they all owe you a lot, that's all," Maddy continued. "But you'd never know it from the way they treat you. Maybe it's just me. . . ."

"They're my friends," Charlotte replied defensively, sticking up for them. "We've been through a lot together."

"Close friends?" Maddy asked, her voice becoming a little raspy. "Really? You could have fooled me."

Charlotte was silent.

"I'm going to sleep. Good night, Charlotte."

Charlotte didn't really hear her. She was too busy trying to cope with the feelings of insecurity Maddy had just uncorked.

As Maddy rested, Charlotte floated down from her top bunk and took a seat in one of the uncomfortable chairs next to the large window. She could see the housing developments below and the fence, but everything outside the fence was at a sharp downward angle, descending from the campus, as if they were living at the top of a steeple. It would have been nice to get some fresh air, but not even a supernatural being could pry those windows open.

She started to question herself, focusing on her flaws, magnifying them, like pimples in an unforgiving cosmetics mirror. Wasn't she supposed to be past all this stuff? Transformed somehow from the geeky loser she had been to the wise and wonderful spirit she had become. Just now, she wasn't feeling

very . . . evolved. She looked over at Maddy and was unnerved by her wide-eyed expression.

"Mind closing your eyes? I don't really want to deal with the whole 'vacant stare' thing right now."

"Per your request," Maddy said sleepily as she took her fingers and manually closed her eyes.

Maddy was definitely different from the other girls, but at least she was there. To Charlotte, that meant a lot. Everyone else was too busy working or being reunited or whatever. She closed her own eyes and fell asleep.

＄

The morning sun had broken through the gloom for the first time since she'd been there, and Charlotte took it as a positive sign.

"C'mon, Maddy," Charlotte hollered down the hallway with some frustration. "We're going to be late."

She'd been standing there holding her finger on the elevator button for who knows how long, and she could just imagine the choice words the tenants on the floors above and below were having for her right now. In fact, she didn't need to imagine as the unkind phrases began floating up through the shaft and into the car.

"Not exactly the best way to make friends," she said aloud.

She began to think about all the morning rituals she remembered from her Life. No matter how eager she ever was to leave her home, whichever one she'd been placed in that year, waking up was always such a chore, she recalled.

At least one upside of death was that all the inconveniences demanded by good hygiene could be sidestepped forever.

There was no more wiping sleep out of her eyes, washing her face, brushing her teeth, weighing in on a foot scale that was always five pounds off — at least that is how she preferred to see it. No more agonizing over what outfit or hairstyle to wear. No more fearing the bathroom mirror or the full length, for that matter; no more obsessing over how to cover that day's blackhead with pancake makeup, which only drew more attention to it anyway, and then remembering to strategically place her hands over it when she talked to someone up close. Clear the face, clear the air. In fact, Charlotte thought, reaching with her free hand for her face and rubbing her permanently smooth, pale complexion, death was a terrific cleanser. Too bad you couldn't bottle it.

Charlotte poked her head out of the elevator and started to yell down once more when she saw Maddy pop through the apartment door cheerily.

"Nice to see you again," Charlotte said sarcastically, releasing the door button just as Maddy stepped through the portal.

"What's the rush? What are they gonna do, fire us?"

"That's not the point."

"Then what *is* the point?" Maddy asked, her tone of voice cooling in a way Charlotte hadn't experienced before. "It's not like *your* phone is ringing off the hook."

Now there was an observation Charlotte could have done

without. It was pretty irritating not getting any calls, but so far, all the interns had at least had the decorum not to rub it in her face.

As the girls arrived at the phone bank, sounds of displeasure filled the air.

"Usher!" Mr. Markov shouted. "You're late!"

"Busted," Maddy giggled, ducking behind Charlotte and crawling over to her desk, out of the office manager's sight.

Charlotte looked behind her for some support but Maddy was long gone. Pam, Prue, and the others picked their heads up from their calls momentarily and looked over at her, shaking their heads. Charlotte slowly made her way to Markov's office and prepared for the very public blamestorm she knew was coming.

"Aren't we all *late* here," Charlotte joked, trying her best to redirect the abuse.

"This is getting to be a habit," Markov chided, not at all amused. "One you need to break right now."

"We were just, ah . . ."

"People are counting on you, Usher." Markov interrupted loudly. "You are letting them down."

Charlotte wasn't sure exactly who it was she might be letting down, her co-workers or her callers, since neither seemed to be paying much attention to her. Markov was definitely paying attention, however, and he was serious as a heart attack. Judging by his expression, he looked like he might be about to have one. The best move, she decided, was just to go along and not ask too many questions.

"Yes, sir," she responded in an almost clipped, military cadence. The only thing missing was the salute.

Markov stared her down and decided she was sincere.

"Don't let it happen again," he said sternly.

Charlotte shrunk away from him and backed down the corridor, inadvertently smacking into Pam's desk just as she was ending a call.

"What's up with you?" Pam asked, surprised at Charlotte's uncharacteristic nonchalance. "I think that new girl is rubbing off on you."

"Her name is Matilda Miner," Charlotte said peevishly. "And at least she's close enough to rub."

"What do you mean 'close enough'? I'm your best friend over here."

"What did you do last night?" Charlotte asked, seemingly out of the blue.

"Ah, nothing much," Pam paused, giving it some thought. "Mr. Paroda came over to give me my piccolo lesson and Prue, Abigail, and Rita happened to stop by. It turned into a little recital."

"Sounds like fun," Charlotte said dismissively. "Sorry I missed it."

"Charlotte, c'mon. It's not like that. I know you're frustrated about not getting calls and all the reunions, but that's not our fault."

"You know what I did last night? I stared up at the ceiling from my bunk."

Charlotte swiveled her head around and stared at all the

interns eavesdropping on her bitch session with Pam. As she did, each of them lowered their eyes and pretended to be working. All except for Maddy.

"Not that you really care," Charlotte moaned to Pam and walked over to her desk. "Any of you."

Chapter 3

Bad Connection

Fantasy love is much better than reality love.
—Andy Warhol

The idea of someone can often be much more attractive than the reality of that person.

―――――◆―――――

That's why long-distance relationships work. Your idealized romance remains untainted by bad breath, bad habits, and embarrassing parents. Your so-called soul mate is always the person you'd wanted and wished for. The major drawback is, your soul mate is never around. Trouble really starts when the long-distance relationship you are having happens to be with your own feelings.

t Hawthorne High, Charlotte's best living friend, Scarlet, could barely keep her eyes open during last period history. After fidgeting with her vintage specs, she started pulling out wayward threads from her self-silkscreened *Lick the Star* tee while the marching band rehearsed a horrible rendition of Nick Cave's *Do You Love Me?* She gave them points for desperately trying to make the trombone sound like his vocals, but after a while, it all started to give her a headache.

Mr. Coppola, her well-groomed, single, forty-something teacher, who still lived with his widowed mother, was reliving yet again the most interesting experience in his life: his appearance as a teenager on *Let's Make a Deal*.

"Okay, people. Since you've all aced your pop quizzes yesterday, let's just sit back and relish our successes, shall we?" Mr. Coppola said.

He motioned for the door to be opened as if he were going to unleash some sort of "Oprah's Favorite Things" giveaway. Everyone let out a moan of recognition. They all knew what came next.

"What's behind door number one?" he exclaimed as Sam Wolfe, practically on cue, wheeled in a rickety steel A/V cart with a dusty old TV on it. It's as if they'd rehearsed it, and knowing Mr. Coppola as Scarlet did, this was not an unreasonable assumption. Still, she was always happy to see Sam.

"Do we have to watch Howie Mandel again?" a boy in the back shouted.

Mr. Coppola spun around as tightly as a professional ice skater and ran up to the boy.

"Howie Mandel?" he raged in disbelief. "It's Monty Hall! There's no comparison. Monty Hall is a legend — the gold standard of game show deal making."

Mr. Coppola's face had turned apple red by now, his eyes bulging and a faint lisp detectable through his tirade. He was tightly wound, Mr. Coppola was, and seeing who could raise his blood pressure to the boiling point had become a sport for every class since he'd come to Hawthorne. The most direct route was a full-frontal onslaught of Monty Hall.

"Now be quiet, and try to learn something," he ordered, signaling Sam to begin.

The static-y third generation videotape rolled, and Mr. Coppola watched intently, waiting to see *himself.* Everyone sat there in the dark, watching the screen and waiting for Mr. Coppola to shout, "There I am!" And right on schedule, at seven minutes in, a young, mustachioed Mr. Coppola —

dressed in a Xanadu T-shirt, tight running shorts, knee-high tube socks, and Adidas sneakers — appeared, for exactly two seconds, right behind Monty Hall, who was, as always, making a deal with some rube who couldn't decide between a Cadillac and a donkey.

Seeing himself always triggered a pause on the tape and a story of how he had the Q-tip in his pocket, but the woman in front of him couldn't make a deal because she didn't have one. He then would get swept away by the way Monty Hall tilted his head to acknowledge him when he walked up the steps toward the woman. He thought, as everyone else surely did in the auditorium, that Monty was headed directly to him. For those few seconds, he thought he would be . . . chosen.

Scarlet tried to pay attention, even taking in the whole *Let's Make a Deal* as Metaphor-For-Life, but she was worlds away. She and her boyfriend, Damen, had been on the phone all night talking endlessly about independent movies, new music downloads they wanted to check out, and concerts that they wanted to go to. She was a different person when she talked to him. Open and chatty, her sentences would unspool breathlessly. The adrenaline rush was so strong it would take her hours to fall asleep after they hung up, if she slept at all.

She was exhausted because, sadly, she wasn't used to late nights like that anymore. With Damen away at college, and Scarlet working and finishing high school, it was getting really hard to find time for each other. Or, in her mind at least, it was getting harder for him to find time for her. Visits home and even phone calls had become more and more infrequent. They were in different places now, in more ways than one, and

Scarlet was feeling that the distance between them was about more than miles.

Besides, she really missed him. They'd shared things together that she couldn't, wouldn't, have shared with anyone else in their little deadbeat town. Damen always made sure to share every single detail of bands he'd seen at The Itch and movies that played off campus, saving promotional mementos like posters and ticket stubs and snagging her some T-shirts from the groups that were playing in his cool college town, a world away from Hawthorne. At least he did for a while, she thought.

Scarlet was not naïve. She knew the dangers of not being together, not making new memories. It was death to a relationship. And if the end of last night's conversation was any indication, she decided, the patient was sick.

"Well, I better let you go," she recalled Damen saying. "You have to get up early for school. . . ."

He wasn't exactly rushing her off the phone, but the passive construction of his goodbye, and seemingly generous tone — wrapping his signoff in a condescending little verbal pat-on-the-head — she thought analytically, might be hiding a deeper truth. He didn't say, "I have to go." He said, "I'll let *you* go. . . ." In other words, putting the burden of ending the call on her, leading her to believe it was her decision when it wasn't. *She* wasn't done with the call, but apparently, *he* was.

Hang-ups were always awkward between them anyway, but why couldn't he just say what he meant? This led her to the most worrying issue of all.

They had never said "I love you." Not on the phone, not in

person. They'd gotten close, but had never actually spoken the words. This troubled Scarlet because they'd been together for some time and surely each knew how the other felt, but neither could muster up the courage to say it first. Well, that was her take on it anyway.

Could it be he didn't say it because he didn't feel it? So much had changed in their lives over the past year. It would certainly be understandable for his feelings to have changed. Or maybe they had passed the point of saying it, which would be even worse. That would mean their relationship was just moving along on auto-pilot or . . . on fumes.

Her sister, Petula, who was prone to giving Scarlet little hurtful jabs in the guise of sisterly advice, had implied that maybe Scarlet's relationship was just a *fauxmance* and that Damen had moved on while Scarlet was just a stupid, little school girl chasing after him. Scarlet knew exactly what Petula was trying to do. She was still carrying the torch for Damen, not to mention nursing the huge blow to her ego from when he dumped her for her little sister. That much was obvious, but her digs definitely let a little more doubt creep in.

When the loudest voice in your head is Petula, Scarlet thought, you know it is time to stop thinking. All this emotional excavation was very out of character for a head as cool as Scarlet's, so before she posed any further threat to her own sanity, she took a deep breath and recalled what Damen had actually *said*, and not what she *heard*.

"I . . . love . . . you know . . . talking to you" were his exact words last night.

"That wasn't soooo bad, was it?" Scarlet reprimanded

herself, embarrassed at the ride she'd just taken on the crazy train.

"Well, I'm glad you aren't just in it for my fame, body, and money," Scarlet recalled joking, trying to take some of the tension off the wrap-up. Damen laughed for a second, then she heard a click in her ear, and the line went silent.

ॐ

Scarlet's big sister suffered from no such internal conflicts. Petula's only debate that day was whether to sign in to school and then skip out for a pedicure at the Korean day spa or to just cut totally and give in fully to her need to primp. She was leaning toward the second option, not just out of irresponsibility but out of pure indifference. School had never meant much to her, except as a place to validate her superiority, and it meant even less now that she had been left back. The Fall Ball incident had mostly faded from Hawthorne High's collective memory, but Petula was still being made to pay for her crime via an involuntary senior year do-over. Typically, however, she found the silver lining in this humiliating cloud and exploited it to her advantage.

In fact, getting left back turned out to be a blessing in disguise for her. She much preferred being a big fish in a little pond, and the prospect of starting her social climb all over again at some junior college was unappealing. She had few skills and fewer ambitions. She didn't really *mean* anything outside of high school and she knew it. Her best friends, the Wendys, soaring to new heights of superficiality, held them-

selves back too, in sort of an homage to Petula. So, despite the setback, not much had changed for Petula.

Today's pedicure was an urgent matter. She was beautifying for her big date with a younger man, Josh Valence — a senior from Gorey High — Hawthorne High's biggest rival. Josh was the captain of their football team and quite a catch, so she wanted to be super perfect from head to toe. Snagging a jock was only half her motivation, however, the other half was revenge. She hoped that word would get back to Damen. He'd lost the big game last year to Gorey in a squeaker, and even though Damen never gave it a second thought, Petula, in her infinite pettiness, imagined that dating Josh would really eat him alive.

By the time she'd completed the parts of her beauty regimen she could manage on her own, she was already running behind schedule. She arrived a few minutes late to the day spa and was livid to find that despite the emergency appointment she'd made the night before, she still had to wait. She watched the seconds tumble away, drops of sweat popping through her cleansed pores and beading on her plucked brows.

She still had to go to the tanning salon, get back home, eat a few carrot sticks, shower, set her hair, and steam her new bra-tank, not to mention pick up Scarlet from school since she had borrowed her car, all while texting the Wendys her every move. She was stressing big-time, although the "picking up Scarlet" item in her daybook was very low priority.

She'd been waiting three whole minutes before she took her place on the pedicure throne and her nail tech began to scrub,

scrape, pumice, massage, and clip. Ordinarily Petula would have required executive treatment and would never have bothered to speak to the help. But today she was growing more and more impatient and rushing the whole process.

"What are you doing?" she snapped. "I don't want my cuticles pushed back."

The nail tech looked up at her with a smile and resumed her work. Petula thought that she wasn't getting it.

"Don't you talky American? Me No Likey!" she railed ignorantly while pushing back the cuticles on her fingers as a kind of sign language. The tech nodded again, blankly this time, and Petula exploded.

"Chop, chop," Petula bullied, again urging the tech to pick up the pace, her agitated feet splashing dirty water, flakes of dried skin, calluses, and toe jam all over the girl.

When her need for speed was still unacknowledged, Petula went totally Rocky 1 on her.

"Cut me!" she finally roared, pointing to her toenails.

The girl was moving as quickly as possible, trying her best to meet all of Petula's demands, but with her hands nervous and shaking, she accidentally nicked Petula's big toe.

Petula continued screaming at the girl and broadcasting her incompetence to the whole spa, so much so that people and clinicians were peeking their heads out of waxing rooms to see what all the commotion was about.

"Here, let me put some alcohol on it," the girl said apologetically in perfect English, which made Petula even madder.

"I think you've done enough," Petula barked. "This better NOT scar!"

Petula grabbed her things, hobbled outside still wearing her paper flip-flops and foam toe separators, and jumped in the car.

She was already pissed enough, but having to drive home in Scarlet's dented and scratched jalopy, plastered with band and radio station bumper stickers and a hubcap-less spare tire, was almost unbearable. And the car was black, her least favorite color.

Petula usually wore a scarf on her head, oversized glasses, and, on occasion, a wig to disguise herself whenever she had to drive it. More than anything, the car reminded Petula of Scarlet, providing plenty of reason for her to hate it.

She pulled up to the school and rolled down the passenger window just as Scarlet emerged. Scarlet was mortified to hear the new Fergie CD blasting over her mint soundsystem and prepared for battle.

"Get in, Little Miss Misery," Petula ordered as she saw Scarlet emerge from school.

The first thing Scarlet noticed was Petula's paper flip-flops.

"I see you've had a productive day," Scarlet said sarcastically. "You can't drive with those things on. They don't constitute as shoes."

"Aw, does somebody have a case of 'the sads'?" Petula asked, dripping with phony sympathy. "You are making me late for a very important date."

Scarlet ran through a million comebacks in her mind, like how Petula was an irritating polyp on the butt of society, but uncharacteristically let it slide instead. She bit her lip and kept

silent. The ride home felt like ages to Scarlet, but Petula actually made it home in record time. The car had barely stopped when Scarlet threw open the door like a kidnapping victim and literally jumped out. It wasn't a "tuck and roll" situation, but nearly.

"I've gotta get ready for work," she yelled as she raced for the front door and up the stairs to her room.

Petula walked in behind her and realized she was almost out of time. She pulled the separators from between her toes and jammed her foot into a pair of the hottest pointy-toed cougar heels she could find in her closet, then sat down on the carved bench in her foyer to wait for Josh.

Before long, a car pulled up and Petula, feeling tired from rushing and verbally abusing nail technicians, kept Josh waiting just long enough to be irritating, as was her trademark. Scarlet emerged from her room wearing her trademark red lipstick, a fitted Slits tee with some black skinny jeans accessorized with a thick, vintage aborigine belt and leopard print flats.

"Oh, look, your hookup is here," Scarlet said as she grabbed her keys and headed out.

Petula waited a few seconds and then strutted catlike down the sidewalk and got in Josh's car. She gave him a long, intimate kiss, said hello, and they sped off. They ended up at a Gorey High house party, a place where Petula was either unknown or loathed. The only person she knew there was Josh, and he was too busy basking in the glow of his super popularity, air-guitaring riffs, and downing Purple Monsters to spend much time with her.

Petula's sourpuss was making it totally clear to Josh that she was unhappy being put in a corner with the other "dates." She wasn't even trying to socialize with any Gorey girls. Josh walked over to give her some face time.

"Hey, so sorry, Petunia," Josh slurred with oily insincerity.

Even as he was chatting to her, Josh was shoulder surfing, his eyes wandering around the crowd to see if he was making any of the other girls jealous or if there was anyone better out there to hook up with. That kind of shopping around really rankled Petula, even more than getting her name wrong.

"Done getting your, ah, ego stroked by your *Bromeos?*" Petula cracked.

"I'd rather you stroke it," Josh said, putting his hands around her waist.

Petula saw his lips moving but could barely hear him through the crowd noise. She really wasn't feeling well all of a sudden. All that self-absorbed small talk from Josh was starting to make her nauseated.

Before Josh could get another uncaring word out, Petula lost her balance and leaned into him. She was looking sick, but Josh misunderstood and thought he was about to score with Hawthorne's most in-demand babe.

"That's more like it," he said cheesily.

"I don't feel good," Petula moaned weakly, leaning harder into Josh for support.

"Oh, yes, you do." Josh whispered as he reached down and squeezed her ass. "You feel great. Wanna get out of here?"

Petula was barely able to shake her head "yes" let alone break his grip on her backside. They split immediately, Josh

flashing a thumbs-up to his drooling teammates and dragging Petula along after him. He was planning to take her to The Hut, which was really just his Dad's ice fishing cabin about five miles away. There were actually beds lined up to accommodate as many couples as possible, like a Third World clinic without the mosquito netting. Unfortunately for Josh, they never made it.

About halfway there, Petula, who had been slumped in the passenger seat practically unconscious, sat upright and puked all over the dashboard, Josh, and herself.

"Holy shit," Josh ranted unsympathetically, dripping vomit. "No wonder Damen left you for your sister."

Petula couldn't hear him. She was nearly passed out completely. Josh swerved into a U-turn and raced back to Petula's house. He screeched to a halt in front, ran around the passenger side, opened the door, and pulled Petula out. He dragged her a few feet and dumped her like a smelly pile of trash on her driveway, then sped off. Petula felt the cold blacktop and little pebbles and gravel pushing into the side of her perfect profile.

Meanwhile, Scarlet, tired from a busy night at the coffeehouse and still a little depressed, drove home immediately after work, anxious to see if Damen had e-mailed. She parked her car on the street and walked over the lawn to the front door. By chance, she looked over at the driveway and thought she saw a sack of garbage.

"Damn raccoons," she muttered, feeling obliged to stomp over and pick it up.

At closer inspection, she saw it was Petula lying there

passed out, her arms and legs splayed. On any other night, she would have just stepped over her, letting her sleep it off in the driveway to teach her a lesson. This time was different for some reason. Even at her worst, Scarlet thought, Petula would never let anyone see her in this condition.

"Party too hard again?" Scarlet asked, nudging her sister gently.

There was no response.

"Petula, wake up," she said, this time louder but not as angrily.

Just then Petula's phone began to ring, only she didn't answer it. Knowing that Petula was a complete nomophobic — in constant fear of being out of mobile phone contact — Scarlet knew then that something was wrong.

She flicked her Bic and knelt down to get a closer look. Scarlet was shocked. Petula's eyes were slightly open and dilated, her breathing shallow. She was drenched in sweat and smelled of vomit. When Scarlet reached to touch her face, it felt like a furnace. She grabbed her sister by the shoulders and turned her over so that they were face to face.

"Petula!" she screamed, over and over, now officially in panic mode. Still no response.

Scarlet rested Petula's back on her lap as she cradled her head, then reached in the pocket of her vintage black, mink-collared coat and called 911.

Chapter
4

Epitaph for the Heart

We don't see things as they are,
we see them as we are.
—Anaïs Nin

You can only get outside yourself by looking inside.

———◆◆◆———

Some people are in constant fear that their heart might cease between beats, feeling each pulse as a countdown to the end rather than a vital sign of life. Others are barely aware that they even have a heart beating inside them, moving through the day unencumbered by the complexity of their inner workings. Worry may not change the outcome, but it definitely affects your outlook. Better to care too much than too little?

**etula was still lying on the gurney** that the EMTs had brought her in on, naked underneath one of those backless white one-size-fits-all surgical gowns. Scarlet rode in the ambulance with her, warding off the PMS — *potential murder suspect* — looks she was getting and nervously watching as the techs checked her vitals and tried to stabilize her. She'd been wheeled through the Emergency entrance of the hospital and into an isolated triage room, away from the rest of the patients being treated in the urgent care rooms.

"What's wrong with her, doctor?" Scarlet pleaded, leaning over Petula's helpless body.

"Right now, I have no idea," Dr. Patrick answered. "All we know for sure is that she is fevered and unresponsive. Comatose, clinically."

Scarlet turned away, petrified at that word, and was relieved

to see her mom rush into the room. She was less pleased to see the Wendys burst in close behind. The look on the Wendys' two faces at the sight of Petula might have been perceived as shock or grief or even sympathy by someone who didn't know them so well, but Scarlet knew better. She knew it was the look of pure jealousy. Though she prided herself on her inability to guess what they were thinking at any given moment, Scarlet rightly assumed the source of their envy was Petula's perfect immobility. They had been auditioning to be body sushi models at the new Japanese restaurant in town, and stillness was a required skill they had yet to master.

"Is she on any medications?" the doctor continued as she proceeded to examine Petula.

"Um, not on a regular basis, no," Wendy Thomas answered, jumping in unwarrantedly.

"No, she's not," Scarlet snapped as she stood next to her mother like a protective tigress. "Isn't this room reserved for family members?"

"We're more like sisters to her than you are, Harlot," Wendy Anderson added. This stung because Scarlet suspected — for better or worse — they were probably right.

Kiki Kensington, Petula and Scarlet's mom, waved them all to shut up. This was serious business and it was instantly clear whom both Petula and Scarlet had inherited their no-nonsense demeanor from.

"Is there a possibility she could be pregnant?" Dr. Patrick asked.

"No. She is NOT pregnant," Mrs. Kensington snipped authoritatively.

"She does look bloated around the middle," Wendy Anderson said to Wendy Thomas out of the side of her mouth while tapping her own six-pack for signs of flab.

"Yeah, knocked out *and* knocked up," Wendy Thomas jabbered.

"Well, the truth is, doctor, we really can't be sure if she's pregnant or not. I mean, she did have a hot date with Josh last night," Wendy Thomas said, evaluating evidence with all the skill of an online college C.S.I. grad. "So I don't think any of us have the authority to officially deem her barren."

Scarlet rolled her eyes and silenced the Wendys with a look that would have melted the polar ice caps faster than global warming. She was so not into these catty dimwits spreading a pregnancy mystery of Princess Diana proportions around Hawthorne with Petula laid up and totally defenseless.

"I'm sorry, but we need to ask this of all females of child-bearing age before we can administer any treatment or medications," Dr. Patrick added kindly for Mrs. Kensington's sake. "It's protocol. We'll confirm it with a blood test anyway. Why don't all of you go out and take a little break? It may be a while before her labs come back. We will call you if there's any change."

Mrs. Kensington walked outside to call her ex-husband, with Scarlet close behind. Scarlet watched her dial and was a little shocked. She didn't even know her mom still had his

number. Tragedy and sickness had a strange way of bringing people together, she thought. Even bitter exes.

For some reason, overhearing that call made her think of Charlotte and her memorial photo in the school paper. No one from Charlotte's family was there, she remembered. Didn't she have anyone who missed her, she recalled thinking as she typed up the obituary? Anyone who cared?

Scarlet hugged her mom and headed toward the elevator as she tried to reach Damen on his cell. His phone kept responding "out of the area" so she couldn't even leave a message. She didn't feel comfortable texting him the details of what was happening. She needed him so much right now and he was unavailable.

While Mrs. Kensington and Scarlet headed out, the Wendys lingered behind.

"Ah, doctor, one more thing," Wendy Anderson interjected just as the doctor was leaving. "You can't catch a coma, can you?"

The doctor ignored the question and thrust the sterile blue curtain shut on the threesome.

The Wendys looked at each other and immediately pulled out their iPhones. They started an impromptu Facebook photo shoot, posing alongside Petula's unconscious body. Wendy Anderson tilted Petula's head up close to hers while Wendy Thomas stood on a chair, trying to get the highest overhead angle possible, and snapped the pictures.

"We are gonna get so many hits. Send out a new photo alert!" Wendy Thomas exclaimed as they insensitively swung their PDAs around like flashlights in a dark cave, searching

for a wi-fi signal that would allow them to upload their new content.

ஐ௸

The Wendys got the hits they were looking for, and word got out that Petula was in the hospital almost instantly as a result. Guys from her class began making the pilgrimage to the hospital once the Wendys' Web site crashed from too many visitors. Not to give support or show respect, but to get a first-hand look at Petula Kensington, unconscious, in bed, and practically nude. It was their collective lifelong dream.

"Name?" the older receptionist at the nurses' station asked.

"Burns, Richard," a guy replied as Scarlet passed by.

The receptionist typed his name on an ID sticker.

"Nice try, Dick Burns. . . . Like no one has ever heard that one before," Scarlet snapped as she ripped the identity tag off his American Eagle jacket.

The receptionist looked confused.

"They are trying to eye-hump her," Scarlet raged, angry at both the slobbering guys and the clueless receptionist. "*My sister* isn't taking visitors, just close friends and family on the list we provided. It's in the computer."

A long line of guys sighed in unison and turned away as Scarlet continued out the glass doors.

She quickly turned her back and speed-dialed Damen again. She was desperate for support and, most of all, guidance. Her call was interrupted by her call waiting beep. She took the phone away from her ear and looked at the face. It was a text message. She eagerly clicked to open it. It wasn't

from Damen, after all, but rather a message from her mom. It said that the doctor was back and that she needed Scarlet to get back to the room.

Scarlet didn't even wait for the elevator, instead, she ran up four flights of steps in a matter of seconds.

"Can we get a softer bulb in this thing?" Wendy Thomas asked a nurse checking Petula's chart while holding up Petula's lamp. "It's really harsh and it makes her pores look *huge!*"

Scarlet and her mother walked in the room, holding hands, unified against whatever news would come. Dr. Patrick entered just behind them. She began immediately in that neutral matter-of-fact tone that doctors affect whenever the news is not good.

"We've ruled out several things based on the results of her bloodwork, one being a small cyst on her ovary that we thought might have ruptured and caused an infection."

"A cyst? My aunt had a cyst and it had teeth! Not just like front teeth, but molars!" Wendy Anderson said, fighting back a deposit of her stomach contents. Still, if Petula had a cyst, they both secretly wanted one too.

"But her white blood cell count is dangerously elevated and her fever is raging," Dr. Patrick mumbled, ruling diseases out or in, as she examined Petula more closely. "Something so acute would have to have a recent cause. . . ."

With that, Dr. Patrick pulled the sheet down further, revealing Petula's feet.

"You took off her new Chanel nail polish!" Wendy Anderson exclaimed. "She's gonna be pissed. You can't even find that shade on eBay anymore!"

Normally Scarlet would have bounced the Wendys out of the room a long time ago, but in an odd way, their shallow comments were comforting now. Scarlet stood there cringing at her sister, partially exposed, being poked like a med school cadaver, and stripped of her polish as well as her dignity.

"That's it!" the doctor said, pointing to her nail.

"Uh-oh . . ." Both Wendys, Scarlet, and Kiki gulped hard in unison.

"Your daughter has contracted a staph infection" — Dr. Patrick squinted and moved in closer to one of Petula's big toes — "from her recent pedicure."

"She wasn't drunk?" Scarlet asked.

"No, she was losing consciousness, and if it weren't for you rushing her here, she might not have made it," Dr. Patrick said, tucking her long ash blond bangs behind her ear.

"See that little cut on her toe — that's where the infection got in," Dr. Patrick said. "Those nail salons are not safe and certainly not sterile."

"It's Pearl Harbor all over again," Wendy Thomas erupted in a bigoted shriek. "A sneak attack!"

"I told her not to go to that salon," Wendy Anderson continued. "I heard that Kim Makler lost her big toe there and now she can't wear any strappy heels this spring."

"Is she going to be all right?" Mrs. K asked, completely oblivious to the Wendys' ridiculous comments.

"The next twenty-four hours will tell us more," Dr. Patrick responded, ordering the nurse to triple the antibiotic dose Petula was receiving.

Scarlet looked over and saw the Wendys' "concern" as a new

pic line was inserted, but she suspected they were just happy to be involved in such a dramatic situation. Being this close to Petula at possibly the hour of her demise would put them in line to inherit her position, her "it-ness." This could make their high school careers and establish a new legacy for them as leaders, not followers. High school, after all, was a game of every girl for herself.

"Don't go shopping for a Louis Vuitton casket cozy just yet," Scarlet quipped. "She's gonna be fine."

The Wendys left the room, and then just as quickly re-grouped, discussing fantasy funeral arrangements and where they would shop for their couture mourning attire.

"Everyone shows grief in their own way." Dr. Patrick shrugged upon their exit. "I guess."

Scarlet put her arms around her mother.

"Actually, this is a critical time. There is nothing more we can do but wait," Dr. Patrick said, causing Mrs. K to break down into tears.

Scarlet made a promise to be there for her mother to lean on, but whom would Scarlet have to lean on? Damen was still out of touch, in every conceivable way.

❧

Kiki definitely needed Scarlet, but Petula, she decided, needed her more. After picking up a change of clothes at home, Scarlet kissed her mom and reassured her. Before she could get out the door, her mom stopped her and reached into the hall closet.

"Please take this with you," Kiki asked through a voice

made hoarse from nonstop sobbing. "She'll need it when she wakes up."

Scarlet wasn't the sentimental type, but she felt tears coming on as she gently took Petula's Homecoming gown from her mother's hand. It was beautifully detailed, specially made just for her. Feeling the fabric run through her fingers, Scarlet understood for the first time why Homecoming was so important to Petula. Why she had gone to such lengths to rebuild her reputation and her voting constituency in the past year. Petula not only wanted to be Homecoming queen — she *needed* to be. Scarlet didn't say another word.

When she arrived at the hospital she carried it in and hung it where Petula could "see" it, just as her mom had requested. It might not have had any effect on Petula's condition right then, but seeing it definitely made Scarlet feel better. Exhausted, she plopped down on the chair, took off her Rockabilly trench, balled it up as a pillow, and slowly fell asleep.

❧

The sound of shuffling feet woke Scarlet suddenly. They were too heavy to belong to the nurses or aides, she thought. She opened her eyes and tried to focus.

"Where have you been?" Scarlet asked, lifting her head from the olive green pleather hospital room recliner. She stood up and walked to the familiar figure in the doorway.

"What do you mean?" Damen said quietly, hugging her tightly enough to almost make her forget her troubles. "I just got back in town and rushed right over."

Scarlet still wasn't sure if she was dreaming or not, but if it was a dream, it was a good one.

"I've been trying to reach you since last night," she rambled. "I called and called, but your cell phone said out of the area, and it kept going to voicemail . . ."

"Well, why didn't you just leave a message for me?"

"And you were in such a rush to get off the phone the other night," she went on. Before she went any further, she hit the brakes and just flat-out admitted, "I thought, maybe, you just didn't want to talk to me."

"Why would you think that?" Damen asked.

But the look of distress on Scarlet's face was so pronounced now that he knew the answer to that specific question was not important.

"I didn't call because I was in the library cramming for a test," he explained. "And" — he paused — "I was coming home anyway."

"Coming home?" she asked.

"For Homecoming, to surprise you," Damen said as he hugged her again. "I know it's not your thing, but I missed you so much."

No kidding, Scarlet thought to herself.

"I went straight to your house and your mom told me what was going on," Damen explained, bug-eyed. "I couldn't believe it."

He had every right to be stunned, everybody was, but Scarlet was trying to decipher from the tone of his voice whether Damen was expressing simple astonishment, or feel-

ing something more, something deeper, like, oh, sympathy, regret, or . . . rekindled love. This was so not like her that she made a conscious effort to get out of her head and back into the conversation.

"Mom's a wreck," she said. "She's in such denial she won't even come here until the news is better."

"Yeah," Damen laughed nervously. "She had all Petula's shoes out and she was polishing them when I got there."

"Last night she was lining up all her fake eyelashes and press-on nails in size order," Scarlet confided. "She's lost it and I'm not far behind, to be honest."

This offhand confession to Damen was the first time Scarlet had spoken out loud about her feelings for Petula's plight, and the fact that the words had come out of her mouth frightened her. He held her close again, brushed the hair from her puffy eyes, and after a minute, they both walked into the hospital room. Damen pulled the blue curtain back and looked Petula over — studied her was more like it. Scarlet watched his every move for telltale signs of revived passion. She couldn't help herself.

This was the first time he'd seen her in ages. Since the Fall Ball last year, when she'd flipped out. He'd been sort of preparing himself to see her at Homecoming. But seeing her like this was sad. If Petula was anything she was proud, and though she probably wouldn't mind being on display, she would totally chafe at being so available.

"What happened?" Damen asked.

"The doctors say she got an infection from a pedicure,"

Scarlet explained. "The one she *wouldn't* have gotten if she wasn't going on a date with Josh . . . the date she wouldn't be going on if I hadn't taken her boyfriend."

"You're not really blaming yourself for this, are you?" Damen asked her gently.

That was nice of him to say, but how could she *not*, Scarlet thought?

Petula was at death's door and there were probably a million medical reasons why, but for Scarlet, the only relevant cause was her own selfishness. The doctors wouldn't find it in the *Merck Manual,* but she was the reason.

Damen walked over, picked up Petula's limp hand, and held it in his. It hurt Scarlet to see him standing there so concerned. He fixed the blue blanket and looked at all the machines. He then brushed Petula's hair out of her face, gently, just as he had hers. Scarlet wanted to get up and leave the room, but she didn't. Petula and Damen had a history together and nothing was going to change that. If he *didn't* care about her, what would that say about him as a person, Scarlet thought?

"She's gonna be okay," Damen reassured Scarlet, his voice wavering.

"I don't know," Scarlet sighed.

"What are the doctors saying? Are they good doctors?" Damen asked, fighting back tears.

"There's nothing more that can be done for her," Scarlet said, also fighting back tears — not only for Petula, but for herself as well. "We just have to wait."

Damen turned to Petula and started to reminisce about

their past. He tried everything to bring her back, just the way you are supposed to when someone is comatose. For Scarlet, sitting there listening, his memories seemed a little too fresh. Too vivid.

"Hey, remember when you said you'd rather be dead than have your hair frizzy?" Damen asked desperately, trying to get her to regain consciousness. "Well, it's starting to frizz."

Scarlet's jealousy was overcome for a minute by the sight of his genuine compassion, the thing she liked most about him.

"Wake up, Petula. I need you . . ." He paused. ". . . to wake up."

Scarlet couldn't stand there and witness such an intimate moment for another second. Whatever her motivation, selflessness or selfishness, didn't matter. She needed to do something to bring Petula back. To restore things to the abnormal, dysfunctional way they had always been. If the doctors couldn't help, she would find a way on her own. She'd only just learned CPR from the poster at Identitea, the cafe at Hawthorne where she worked, but Petula seemed beyond her reach no matter what she might try.

And then it came to her.

Charlotte.

Chapter 5

Dead Sound

*In a manner of speaking
I just want to say
That I could never forget the way
You told me everything
By saying nothing
—Tuxedomoon*

If you can't say something nice, lie.

———◆◆◆———

Words not only help us express emotion, they distance us from it as well. They can be a useful safety net, protecting your heart from overexposure, parceling out your true feelings in carefully crafted syllables rather than gushing sincerity. They can also be misinterpreted, doing damage by creating an impression in someone else's mind that wasn't intended. Sometimes, things really are better left unsaid.

harlotte stepped down the phone bank corridor to chat with Pam, and apologized for her outburst the day before, but Pam was talking away to God knows who and waved Charlotte off. She then turned to Call Me Kim, who was gabbing away as usual. This was definitely heaven to Kim, who had a permanent red-ring phone impression on her face. Just as Charlotte started to trudge back toward her desk, she thought she heard *her* phone ring.

"Omigod, omigod, omigod." Charlotte stopped and shouted out loud, frozen in place at the prospect of getting her first call.

The excitement level in the entire room suddenly jumped too, with all the interns peeking around their cubicles, eyeing one another with relief and urging Charlotte to hurry up and get it.

"Hells Bells!" Metal Mike screeched, his AC/DC fixation still detectable.

"Off the hook," DJ yelled to supportive chuckles from Jerry and Bud.

Charlotte hadn't felt so special since the Fall Ball, and the fact that all this was over a stupid phone call was overwhelming evidence of how much things had changed. Her hesitation delayed her just long enough for Maddy, who was closest to Charlotte's cubicle, to snatch the receiver before the third ring sounded.

"Hello," Maddy answered sweetly, but her expression quickly turned sullen.

Charlotte arrived a second later, anxious to take the call.

"Is it for me?" Charlotte whispered excitedly, bouncing in place on the balls of her feet.

Maddy didn't respond and Charlotte didn't interrupt out of respect for the caller and so as to not distract Maddy. The puckered and serious look on Maddy's face was one Charlotte hadn't seen from her before.

"Maddy?" Charlotte asked more impatiently.

Maddy extended her index finger stiffly and turned her back to Charlotte, the universal sign for "just a minute" or perhaps "this is more important than whatever you have to ask me."

"That could work," Maddy said encouragingly to whomever.

Charlotte could barely hear what she was saying, apart from the fact that Maddy was quickly wrapping up.

Maddy hung up the phone.

"Who was it?" Charlotte asked anxiously. "What'd they want?"

"If you'd been here, you'd know," Maddy chastised. "I'm just glad I was here to cover for you."

"Thank you?" Charlotte said sheepishly, now more cha grined than ever.

"You should know better, Usher," Mr. Markov chimed in. "These calls can be a matter of life and death to someone."

Charlotte frowned and looked up at the video camera above her. Maddy smiled and looked up at the one installed above her. Pam, Prue, and Suzy shook their heads in disbelief and signaled each other to meet in the break room. Charlotte watched them sneak off, but didn't join them.

❧

"That was weird," Pam said, totally immersed in the intern girl talk, sans Charlotte. "Why would Maddy take Charlotte's call?"

"Yeah, she knew how desperate she was to get one," Prue concurred.

"Maybe Maddy was just trying to be helpful," Violet chimed in as Prue's eyes rolled over in disbelief.

"I liked you better when you were mute," Prue snapped.

"You guys are just jealous Charlotte's getting close to Maddy," CoCo added, trying to stir things up as usual.

"Aren't we all supposed to be 'next-leveled,' people?" Suzy Scratcher butted in. "This is all so . . . last life."

"Everyone needs to feel needed, appreciated . . . wanted," Simone purred as Simon shook his black mop in agreement. "Charlotte's feeling lonely."

"This from a pair of twins who tried to out-emo each other!" Prue snapped.

"Look, can't we just get her a call?" Pam chimed in, agreeing with the tragic twins.

"You can't fake a call," Prue barked back, feeling frustrated. "You can't go out and solicit troubled teens!"

"I think we have to trust that this is the way it's supposed to be," Abigail interjected. For Abigail speaking up was rare. She'd lost her confidence when she "dry-drowned" on her own tears after getting dumped by her boyfriend following a swim meet, killing herself and her self-esteem right along with it.

"Easier said than done," Silent Violet said, giving Abigail an encouraging wink as all the girls nodded, broke their huddle, and went back to their cubicles.

ॐ

"Why don't we go home and just hang out?" Maddy said. "You know, have a girls' night."

Charlotte smiled; she was more eager to get out of the sea of phones than ever after another long, uneventful, ringless day.

"I don't know, we're not really supposed to quit early," Charlotte noted, pointing to the video cameras above each of their desks. "And considering how often we've been late . . ."

"Don't worry," Maddy nudged. "It's not like you're missing anything, right?"

"It *would* be more fun than sitting around here, I guess," Charlotte concluded.

Charlotte called out to let everyone know she was leaving. Pam and Prue looked up from their calls and stared at each other, but that was all the reaction Charlotte got. Mike was too busy nearly browbeating some poor caller and rocking air microphone windmills: "You *do not* hope you die before you get old," Mike pushed back. "Trust me, dude." Jerry too was deep in conversation and picking his nails. He flashed them a little peace sign as she and Maddy walked by. Charlotte thought it was sweet of him to acknowledge her exit.

"Peace?" Maddy asked snidely. "How lame."

"Oh, Jerry's sweet," Charlotte said. "He's really nonjudgmental."

"Good thing for him," Maddy said, watching him spit out the last fragment of nail he had been chewing, as she nudged Charlotte out ahead of her.

They walked across the cement courtyard to their apartment building, nodded to the doorman, and headed for the elevators. Just in front of them were a bunch of kids around their age who didn't seem very happy or friendly. Not boisterous like the younger kids were. In fact, they barely looked at Charlotte and Maddy.

The down arrow lit up and the doors opened. Everyone but Charlotte and Maddy got on. The kids turned and stared blankly back at the two girls.

Charlotte looked back at them. Their expressions were sad and forlorn, and Charlotte felt badly for them.

"I guess there isn't room for everyone upstairs," she whispered to Maddy, deciding their problems had to do with room availability.

"Guess not," Maddy said.

As the doors closed, Charlotte watched the passengers drop their heads.

The "up" car arrived just a few seconds later, and Maddy and Charlotte got on and rode it to the seventeenth floor. They both kicked off their shoes and got comfortable.

"So you never really told me how you got here," Maddy asked, quite abruptly, taking a sudden interest in Charlotte's past.

At last, Charlotte thought happily. Someone curious about her, willing to listen to her story.

"Well, I was in love with this guy, or at least I thought so," Charlotte said. "He was so beautiful. So strong and smart and funny. Gorgeous, but if he knew it, he didn't flaunt it."

"What was his name?" Maddy prodded.

"Damen," Charlotte said, releasing his name as if it had been stored away in an old trunk for safekeeping.

"Right," Maddy replied, paying extra-careful attention.

"I died because I was too busy focusing on him and his perfect girlfriend . . . ," Charlotte began.

"Petula," Maddy said, interrupting her.

"How did you know her name?" Charlotte asked quizzically.

"Oh, *everyone* knows her."

"Everyone?" Charlotte pressed, but quickly let it go, figuring it was not really so unusual that Petula would be as well known in the Afterlife as she was in plain old Life.

". . . Anyway I ended up choking to death . . . ," Charlotte said, stopping herself mostly out of embarrassment at having to repeat the whole thing.

". . . On a gummy bear," Maddy said, helping finish her sentence, to Charlotte's surprise. "Your reputation precedes you."

"It does?" Charlotte exclaimed with pleasant surprise, as she experienced a flashback of wanting to be talked about, to be noticed. "Anyway, I struck up a friendship with Petula's sister . . ."

"What was her name?" Maddy asked, wanting to move the conversation along, without Charlotte going off on any tangents.

"Scarlet," Charlotte said, the affection in her voice obvious.

"Tell me more about her," Maddy pleaded. "What was she like?"

"Scarlet is the best friend anyone could ever ask for." Charlotte beamed.

"Oh, you mean like the other interns in the office," Maddy said a bit snidely.

"No," Charlotte said, her eyes wandering and thinking out

loud, "Scarlet is different. I would do anything for her, and I know she would do anything for me."

"Anything?" Maddy asked.

"Anything," Charlotte said firmly, looking her roommate straight in the eyes for maybe the first time ever.

⊙⊙

When times got tough, Wendy Anderson and Wendy Thomas did what they usually did to keep their spirits up — they went shopping and got their hair done. Their nails too. In fact, they went back to the scene of the crime, the same place that Petula went — where tragedy struck. They admired and secretly envied the makeshift memorial of flowers, cards, notes, and balloons that were piled up outside of the salon, not to mention the large number of girls who were turning up in droves to get their nails done in a goodwill gesture of solidarity because, in their minds, if they didn't, the staph would win.

The Wendys needed to prepare for the worst, and if the worst came for Petula, they had to look their best. After getting their nails done and faking fragile emotional states, they headed over to Curl Up & Dye, the most expensive hair salon in town, where they directed the stylists to use two of the greatest fashion funerals of the twentieth century as inspiration.

"I think I'm gonna go vintage mourning," Wendy Anderson decided, experimenting with an Aqua-Netted flip curl and pill box hat. "Assassination-era Jackie O."

"Yeah, grieving first lady is definitely a classic, tasteful

vibe, but I'm thinking more natural, less fuss. More Elvis-dying-on-the-toilet period Priscilla Presley," Wendy Thomas chirped. "I was thinking of stained baby doll dress–fishnets-suicide-era Courtney, but I don't know. Maybe the wrong tone?"

"What was good enough for the King . . . ," Wendy Anderson began.

". . . Will be good enough for the Queen," Wendy Thomas agreed, and went back to admiring her reflection.

Everyone in town was curious about Petula's condition, but this was the first chance anybody actually had to ask one of her confidantes about her. She didn't want to pry, but this was too good an opportunity for the stylist to pass up.

"Are her feet modeling?" one of the Wendy's hair technicians asked indelicately.

"Her feet were never her best asset," Wendy Anderson replied, misunderstanding the question. "Especially now, with the horrible swelling and deadly infection from her big toe raging through her bloodstream."

"No, I mean *modeling* . . . ," the stylist said, making a cupped curl in Wendy's hair, ". . . the way your feet become curled up like this when someone is dying."

"Oh, no. I don't think so," Wendy Thomas responded. "But, then again, her feet are always naturally pointed because of that damn second toe."

"She was thinking of having it fixed before this calamity, but now . . . ," Wendy Anderson, teary-eyed, reported.

Whether the teardrops were welling for Petula or her

Morton's toe or were just practice for the big event was hard to tell.

"What better time than now for a reduction," Wendy Thomas said matter-of-factly. "She's completely out of it, and her heels would fit soooo much better if she's having an open casket."

"Good point, Wendy," Wendy Anderson said. "I'll bring it up. Who do you think has power of attorney?"

The hairdressers were stunned into silence. They couldn't even open their mouths to crack the flavorless gum they'd been chewing. Both resumed their work, reaching for the tweezers, and began plucking the Wendys' eyebrows.

"Hey, can I take a pair of those tweezers?" Wendy Thomas asked. "It's just that the three of us made a pact that if one of us ever became a veggie, we would pluck the random un-wanted hair from her face."

The technician was touched and handed Wendy a spare tweezer. It was a generic stainless steel one, not the hot pink, enameled kind that she was using on the Wendys.

As the Wendys had their brows furrowed into the proper shape, they could see the memorial across the street beginning to grow. It was getting impossible to ignore. Petula would have loved it, which guaranteed that The Wendys, of course, re-sented it. As the hair tech looked over distractedly for just a second to check it out, she lost her place.

"Ow!" Wendy Anderson screamed, pushing the tech's hand away. "You bruised a follicle!"

Wendy Thomas felt a coma coming on and panicked.

"Don't you know these things always happen in threes?" she shouted.

With that, Jackie-redux and Priscilla-lite hurriedly picked up their things and bolted for the door as if the Angel of Death himself were chasing them.

Chapter 6

Girlfriend in a Coma

I can now see everything
falling to pieces before my eyes.
—Ian Curtis

Nobody can have it all.

———◆✦◆———

Thus, jealousy, which is not necessarily such a terrible thing. Jealousy is kind of like an emotional dipstick that tells you how hot you, your wants, your needs, or your relationships are running. A barometer of personal satisfaction. The real issue is whether the jealousy you feel is motivating or crippling. For some people, it's both.

 can't just sit back and watch her like this," Scarlet said, finally getting to her breaking point.

"I know," Damen said, trying to comfort her.

"No, I mean, I'm *not* going to sit back and watch," Scarlet said, rejecting his pity.

"Maybe you should go home and get some rest," Damen said gently, sensing she was on her last nerve. "I'll stay with her."

"I bet you will," Scarlet said under her breath.

"What's gotten into you?" Damen asked.

"These doctors aren't doing jack squat," Scarlet said, her frustration matching her jealousy. "But I've been thinking . . ."

"Uh-oh," Damen said, reacting to the serious look on Scarlet's face.

"There might be a way I can help Petula," she said. "In fact, *I* might be the only one who can."

"How do you propose you're going do that?" Damen was nervous to consider what Scarlet might be contemplating. "She's got the best doctors, specialists, nurses, all doing the best they can."

Scarlet laid it out for Damen.

"If Petula isn't here, where is she?" Scarlet asked.

"But she is here." Damen pointed to the bed, treating Scarlet as if she were a child — or a lunatic.

"Not her body, that's just a shell," Scarlet chided him. "Her mind. Her soul. *Petula.*"

Damen shrugged his shoulders, not quite sure what she was getting at.

"Look, I know 'soul' is a word none of us have ever used in the same sentence as 'Petula,'" Scarlet acknowledged, "but even she has one."

"Okay," Damen answered deliberately, for the sake of argument at least.

"Well, then it has gotta be *somewhere,* right?" Scarlet asked.

"That's a pretty big question," Damen answered, still unsure of where she was going with all of this. "And I just happened to leave my Philosophy 101 textbook at school, so . . ."

"Don't be so narrow-minded," Scarlet said curtly. "You were there at the Fall Ball."

"Yeah, and . . . ," Damen replied incredulously.

"There is a whole other reality we know nothing about," Scarlet reminded him. "Well, obviously, some of us don't, anyway."

With that, she turned her back on Damen and crossed her arms, sulking.

Damen reached for her shoulders and spun her back around with more force than she'd ever felt from him before. He held her tightly and proceeded to get rational.

"I don't know what happened that night," Damen said,

clearly having put much of that evening out of his head. "But whatever it was, it was a fluke. A once-in-a-lifetime thing."

"What if her spirit is dwelling on the other side and it is just a matter of time before she dies and her soul completely separates from her body? Maybe even sending her to Hell for all we know!"

"Scarlet . . . ," Damen said softly.

"Maybe she's in a circling pattern? Waiting to get checked off of a friggin' list or something, and we're just sitting here while she turns into firewood!"

"Scarlet, you need to calm down," Damen said more forcefully this time.

"How do you know what I need?" Scarlet snapped, surprised at what just escaped from her mouth.

Damen was worried. It was not like her to act so erratically, and he was starting to think she might be on the verge of a breakdown.

"I'm sorry," Scarlet said earnestly. "I just want to help Petula. She could be damned for all we know."

Scarlet was not just being dramatic, but she wasn't being entirely honest, with Damen or herself, either. They both knew that Petula hadn't exactly lived an exemplary life and that the odds of a good outcome for her in the Afterlife were slim at best. But Scarlet's concerns were driven less by Petula's spiritual deficiencies than her own guilty conscience.

In her mind, she'd taken Damen away. And on some level it felt good, winning for a change and serving Petula up some just desserts. But the thought of never being able to make it right between them, to apologize, even if she didn't really

regret it, before Petula headed straight to Hell in an oversized handbag, was unbearable.

"We don't know that," Damen uttered reassuringly.

"No, we don't, but I know someone who probably does," Scarlet said, half-hopeful and half-petrified.

"Let me guess," Damen said, finally putting it together. "Charlotte?"

Scarlet was silent.

"How are you going to contact Charlotte?" Damen asked skeptically. "She's . . . gone."

"I'm going to go find her."

"You're not going to start speaking in tongues, are you?"

"I'm serious," Scarlet said soberly. "I'm going over there, Damen."

"I can't let you do that! What if you don't come back?"

"I'm going," Scarlet said firmly.

"What if Petula wakes up?" Damen asked, still trying to convince her to wait it out. "She could at any second!"

"*What if* isn't *what is*," Scarlet said even more definitively.

Damen noticed a sudden calmness and resigned-ness in her expression, the kind of look you see on the faces of martyred saints on those supermarket devotional candles.

"If I can find Charlotte," Scarlet reasoned, "maybe she can help me find Petula. And then we can save her."

Damen held her tight and whispered in her ear.

"What about *you*? Who is going to save you?"

"Oh, Romeo," Scarlet said, trying to lighten the mood. It comforted Damen a bit to know that her sense of humor, if not her sanity, was still intact.

"Scarlet, I'm serious," Damen said sternly. "I know you think you know what you're doing . . ."

"Damen, I've been over there before. If I can help Petula and I don't, I won't be able to live with myself."

For all his levelheadedness, Damen knew she was right. He also knew there was no stopping her now. He'd seen that look before. Her mind was made up.

They looked into each other's eyes as if it might be their last chance. In her eyes he saw resolve, in his she saw respect . . . and fear.

"She would do the same for me," Scarlet said sarcastically, trying to get him to crack a smile.

They both laughed, bonding over Petula's selfishness that they both oddly missed so much.

"There's just two things," Damen said. "How are you going to get there and what happens to your body when your spirit splits?"

"Details, details." Scarlet poo-pooed.

Scarlet paused, lost in thought for a second as she realized she hadn't thought this through very well. Without her soul, her body was very likely to wind up just like Petula, maybe worse.

"Yeah, well, they say that's where the Devil is."

"Have you just met me?" Scarlet asked. "I don't care what people say."

❧

The closet was tiny, definitely not a walk-in, which is what Petula would have insisted on, had she been conscious. It was

overflowing with folded towels, blankets, latex gloves, backless gowns, bedpans, Vaseline, triple antibiotic ointments, bandages, and surgical booties. Barely enough room for supplies, let alone Damen and Scarlet. But it was the only private room available.

He would have much preferred to have snuck into a closet with her for a quick make-out session, but romance was the last thing on his mind, well, one of the last. He was a guy after all.

"Don't worry," Scarlet said in a forceful whisper. "I know what I'm doing."

"Really?" Damen whispered back sarcastically. "What are you going to do, click your Doc Martens three times or something? Scarlet, please don't do this." He was more fragile and open than he had ever been with her. "If anything goes wrong . . ."

"Yes?" Scarlet replied hopefully, breaking her concentration for just a moment, and giving him an opening to declare his undying love.

Damen *wanted* to say he loved her, that he couldn't live without her, but he wouldn't allow himself to get all *Casablanca* with her. It was too maudlin, too final.

"What will I tell your mom?" he asked instead, hugging her tightly.

"That I'll be back," Scarlet said, trying to convince herself of her answer at the same time.

"Promise?"

Those weren't quite the words she was waiting for, but the point was made. Scarlet was getting jelly-legged now and

wanted to start the incantation before her own common sense got the better of her.

"Can you, you know, wait outside?" Scarlet asked Damen apologetically.

"Sure," he agreed nervously. "I'll be right outside."

Damen closed the door and the room was dark. Scarlet shut her eyes and started to hypnotize herself into believing she was with Charlotte. She thought about the first time they met, recalling every single detail — the beakers, the chalk dust, the way Charlotte looked, touching her fragile hands as she recited the incantation with shallow breaths. Soon, she was there. Right there in that moment. It scared her a little, but feeling Charlotte's presence so vividly calmed her.

"You and me, our soul makes three," she said excitedly.

She waited for just a moment — at least, that's how fast she thought it was — and she heard a voice echoing faintly in the distance.

"Me and you, our soul makes two," it whispered in a familiar tone.

"We are me," Scarlet finished, her eyes opening as wide as her mouth.

Damen heard her bumping into shelves, burst into the closet, and was able to catch her just before she hit the floor. Her eyes were blank, her breathing labored, and her skin clammy. It was as if somebody had just hit the "off" switch on her.

Damen quickly pushed open the closet door and shouted for help as if Scarlet's life depended on it. And in some ways, it did.

Chapter 7

Imitation of Life

We are what we pretend to be,
so we must be careful what we pretend to be.
—Kurt Vonnegut

Love and Death have a way of distorting things.

When you fall in love, you see the world through rose-colored glasses. When you pass away, you are viewed through them. In love and death, all faults are ignored or forgiven. You are transfigured, cast as a character in everyone else's biopic of your life.

**etula awoke slowly. She thought she** heard a voice, a male voice, calling to her, but when she opened her eyes, she was completely alone. Her head propped up on a pillow, she reached for her face, checking for any imprints on her cheek from the gravel. It was the last thing she remembered before going to sleep. God forbid she have to deal with pock marks before Homecoming, especially after all the money she'd spent on weekly dermabrasion treatments and collagen-based skin fillers. Still fuzzy, she blinked a few times to get the sleep dirt out of her eyes, looked down, and evaluated herself as she did each day, just to make sure she looked as hot as the day before.

She didn't recognize the sheer poly cotton smock she was wrapped in, but it did look good on her. It really played to her strengths, namely her ass, which was mostly visible. What most people didn't realize, mainly because of her beautiful

face and perfect chest, which drew their eyes upward, was that she had a short torso. This sweet little number she was wearing, however, covered up that minor anatomical hiccup and put the emphasis where it belonged: on her legs, which went on forever — all the way to her feet, in fact. Her feet. The source of all of yesterday's drama that suddenly came flooding back.

"Bitch," she said, squinting for a second to focus on her toes and the unfinished pedicure.

With that little curse-out of the nail tech, Petula was fully roused, or at least enough to recognize that she wasn't in her own bed. Or even at home, for that matter. She sat up, looked around, and swung her legs over the side of the bed, which she could recognize now as a hospital bed from her past mandatory-volunteer work as a candy striper in the geriatric ward.

"What or *who* did I do last night?" she wondered, more curious than afraid.

She couldn't recall much of the date with Josh, but what little she could was not worth the neurons it took to retrieve. Suddenly, she remembered she'd gotten really dizzy and puked. Totally freaked at such inappropriate public behavior, she convinced herself he must have slipped her some kind of date-rape drug.

"Pervert," she thought.

She pushed herself off the bed until her feet reached the floor, and as they did, she felt a twinge. Not pain, exactly, but enough discomfort to notice. She limped gingerly through the empty room toward the door and out into the hallway.

"Hey?" Petula yelled, her voice echoing faintly down the corridor. "Yo Yo Yo?!"

Finally, she called "Holá?" snidely. No response.

She gimped to the nurses' station, which was unmanned as well.

"We really do need health care reform in this country!" she snarled.

Farther down the hall, she could see a cool white light emanating from an office.

"Thank God," Petula said, relieved, heading for the glow.

As she approached the door, she tried to look in, but the glare from the office light that spilled out into the dim hallway distorted her view. Annoyed, but undeterred, Petula pushed the door open and entered in her trademark huff.

"Hello?" Petula called out obnoxiously. "I'm here to be discharged?"

Her greeting bounced off the walls, ceiling, and floor. The office was as empty as the hallways and her hospital room. It wasn't just that there was *no one* there: there was no *thing* there either. No magazines, no instructional pamphlets or paperwork of any kind. It was bare as her bottom, except for a desk with a bell, a chair in the back of the room, and a bench, which ran along the side wall under the windows. On the rear door there was an AUTHORIZED PERSONNEL ONLY sign.

"Hey!" she shouted again as she rang the little bell on the desk repeatedly. "I really don't have time for this today."

Petula was not used to waiting or being unattended to. She turned to the door to leave and noticed another sign hanging from the doorknob.

YOUR TIME IS IMPORTANT TO US, it read. PLEASE NOTIFY

THE RECEPTIONIST IF YOU HAVE NOT BEEN ATTENDED TO
WITHIN __ MINUTES.

The number of minutes she was to wait was not specified
on one of those little clock faces with the plastic hands. Nevertheless, Petula was encouraged that someone was attending
the room and that she would not be kept from her daily schedule much longer.

"That's a good sign," Petula thought, not intending the pun.

She settled herself down and took a seat on the bench. As
her skin hit the hardwood, she felt a little chill for the first
time. She pulled her hospital gown down as low as it could go,
covering her knees, which was almost unheard of for her, and
crossed her arms in front of her to keep the cold away.

"So much for global warming," she theorized.

Before long, however, the loneliness became more of an issue for her than the chill. Solitude, regardless of how brief,
was not good for Petula, and she was self-aware enough to
know it. She was not a very introspective sort in the best of
times, and these were not the best of times.

Though she always displayed complete disdain for the general public, Petula needed people more than she would ever
care to admit. No pressure to actually interact with individu-
als, to give anything of herself, was required. She needed their
attention, their adoration, even their hatred and jealousy.
Large, faceless crowds of worshippers were a particular favorite of hers. Just a perfunctory smile and wave was all it took to
soothe the adoring throng.

Petula held her hand up to her face, out in front of her at
arms length and examined her clear-coat manicure, which had

been completed expertly, unlike her tragic pedicure. Noticing her own reflection in her fingernails, she decided to use this time constructively by practicing her pose down. She spread her digits wide to create as many angles as possible, a slightly different view of herself reflected in each. It wasn't her full-length bedroom mirror, but under the circumstances, it would have to do.

"Glamour shot," she said, turning her profile sharply to her outstretched hand, her other arm turned elbow out and hand placed firmly on her hip.

"Reaction shot." She brought one had to her cheek, rounded her lips and busted a surprised "who me?" expression.

She even practiced being humble and tearing up for what was sure to be her inevitable coronation as Homecoming Queen. After all the humiliation she'd had to suffer at Fall Ball last year, this crowning, in front of the whole school, would be sweet revenge. A return to form. Proof that all was well with the world. The Fall Ball was a big deal, sure, but this was Homecoming! That little "psychotic break" she'd had would be long forgotten once the tiara was placed upon her golden tresses, which was where it belonged, as far as she was concerned.

"What doesn't kill you," she philosophized, stomping her foot for emphasis, "makes you . . . Owwww!"

The pain shot up her leg before she could finish the motivational maxim. It dragged Petula from her imaginary photo session and coronation back to the decidedly less glam environment surrounding her. It was getting noticeably colder now too, and she began to fidget impatiently.

Just then, the front door of the office cracked open slowly.

"It's about friggin' time," Petula bellowed, more relieved for company than she'd ever been before.

The door to the office opened completely, but Petula still couldn't see who was walking in. Whoever it was, she thought, must be vertically impaired or something, because she couldn't see a head through the clear glass window in the upper door.

"Just my luck," Petula moaned, "getting out of here is gonna take forever."

She saw a leg step in, tentatively. It definitely belonged to a little person. But it was a young girl. She poked her head through cautiously, looking at one side and then the other before entering, just as she must have been taught to cross a busy street.

"Where am I?" the girl asked, stepping all the way through the entrance and allowing the door to slowly shut behind her.

That was a very big question, Petula thought, from such a little person, and one she had not the slightest clue how to answer right at the moment.

"And you are?" Petula asked warily of the confused little girl.

"My name is Virginia Johnson," the girl answered, just as skittishly. "What's yours?"

Petula was dumbfounded for a second. It had been a long time since she had needed to introduce herself to anyone, but this was as good a time as any to make an exception.

"*I* am Petula Kensington," she affirmed haughtily, in a tone that might have warranted a curtsy a century or two ago. "Pleased to meet me."

This was Petula's standard M.O. when she was nervous.

Act in a superior and confident way, and the more weak-minded, the more insecure, will buckle. The fact that she would use this tactic on a child was simply an indication of how increasingly anxious she was feeling about everything.

"Let me guess," Virginia said, looking Petula over, "you're a cheerleader."

"How could you tell?" Petula asked with pride.

"Big head to match . . ." Virginia cracked, cocking her neck just slightly to get a better side view of Petula's open-back gown ". . . a big butt."

Petula was not expecting this from such an innocent-looking kid. Her first reaction was to be offended and fire back, but she checked herself instead, sort of charmed by Virginia's spunk. The young girl's fresh mouth also reminded Petula of Scarlet, and all those long car rides they had shared together on summer vacations, before the divorce.

She hadn't thought about those days in a very long time. They'd spent most of the time fighting, sure, but not all the time. They had fun too. Singing out loud until they were hoarse, playing "I Spy" until they were cross-eyed — each seeing things that the other would never notice — and swatting mosquitoes off each other as an excuse to smack one another without getting punished, a game that generally ended in a heated round of "Sudden Death."

Of course it was always a competition between them, and Petula almost always won. If she got the most bites, she used to tell Scarlet it was because "even the bugs couldn't resist" her. Petula was crafty and liked winning, but Scarlet was always the tougher of the two. She would never let Scarlet know, but

Petula would marvel at how her sister could take the abuse, the defeats, and keep coming back for more.

Petula smiled at the little girl she saw in her mind as much as the little girl she saw in front of her.

"You think that's funny?" Virginia chided.

"What?" Petula said distractedly before gathering herself, "Oh, ah . . . no, you just remind me of somebody, that's all."

૭ಿ৩

After shopping, the Wendys arrived at Petula's hospital room, keeping a vigil, some said, or more accurately, a deathwatch, and much to their surprise they saw Scarlet lying just as lifeless in the bed next to Petula. Dr. Patrick was in the room, on evening rounds. Evidence of the commotion was everywhere, with tubes, syringes, tape, gauze, and monitors of all kinds still strewn around from the cardiac team's fight to stabilize Scarlet. Instead of sympathy, all the Wendys could muster for Scarlet was contempt.

"Did she finally see the light and try to kill herself?" Wendy Anderson sniffed.

"Look at that," Wendy Thomas said at the sight of Scarlet lying next to Petula in a hospital bed. "It's booty and the beast."

"What a follower," Wendy Anderson snapped.

"Yeah," Wendy Thomas agreed coldly, "it wasn't enough that she stole her boyfriend. Now she had to go and steal Petula's coma spotlight too?"

Both girls turned suddenly as Damen entered the room. He was rumpled, scruffy, and red-eyed, looking weary and worried. The Wendys, who'd never forgiven him for choosing

Scarlet over Petula — or either of them for that matter — savored this opportunity to kick him while he was down. He ignored them both and took his seat between Petula's and Scarlet's beds.

"What the hell happened?" Wendy Thomas asked, more irate than concerned.

Damen didn't bother to respond. He knew once he got sucked in, he would be caught up in the endless, mindless hamster wheel that was the Wendys' thought process.

"It's possible that Scarlet is in a self-induced coma, triggered by extreme stress," Dr. Patrick said. "It could be psychosomatic."

"You got the psycho part right," Wendy Thomas snipped.

"It might be too much for her to see her sister whom she loves lying there," Dr. Patrick said.

Wendy Anderson was unable to hold back the laughter, and the Red Bull she was drinking leaked out of her nose. The thought of Petula meaning that much to Scarlet was too much for them to handle. However, they managed to regain their composure after Mrs. K, who had been stroking Petula's Homecoming dress absentmindedly, shot them a nasty look.

Just then Scarlet's heart-lung monitor went off, and she appeared to be experiencing some type of acute distress.

"Everybody out," Dr. Patrick ordered and pushed the call button for the crash team. "Now!"

Chapter 8

Back in Your Head

Did I dream you dreamed about me?
—Tim Buckley

Hope against hope.

Most hope is false if you think about it. It's a belief that an outcome will be positive despite evidence to the contrary. But where would we be without it? It's the mind's compass and the heart's buoy, which we cling to as we wait for help to arrive. Without hope, life is sink or swim, and Charlotte hoped she would find a way to swim.

**addy and the others were stuck on** their calls, so Charlotte decided to leave by herself. As she crossed from the office complex to the residential campus, she looked over at the fences that bordered the entire barracks. She hadn't noticed them much before because she'd always been talking to Maddy along the way. They seemed in place more to mark a border than to discourage entry or exit, which made sense. People might have been *dying* to get in, she joked to herself, but no one was too interested in what was on the outside.

Release was becoming a more and more important concept for Charlotte. Her existence had become so burdensome lately that she was actually thinking back fondly on her life — a life that had been marked mostly by insecurity and isolation. Ever since missing that call, in fact, she'd been thinking more and more about Scarlet, Petula, and Damen

and what might have been and about her family and what never was. Most of all she was thinking about what would never be.

Maddy said it. They were seventeen *forever.* That might be an appealing thought for the reality show trophy moms who were always Botoxing, liposuctioning, implanting, and detoxifying to secretly compete for their daughters' boyfriends, but it was increasingly depressing for Charlotte. She'd done everything she was ever going to do, and despite the mark she'd hoped to leave, within a few years' time, her senior picture that was enshrined in the hallway at Hawthorne would inevitably begin to yellow and fade, as would the memory of her. She harbored no illusions about that.

She recalled walking through the cemetery as a kid, looking at the born and died dates on all the tombstones and thinking about the people buried there. She would do the math and calculate how long each person had lived, what they'd seen, and what they'd missed. Electricity, space flight, civil rights, cable TV, the Internet, Starbucks. Some husbands died years before their wives, or children years before their parents. But when you've been dead for a hundred years, let's say, what would it matter if your wife died two years before you? To the passerby, you'd both have been dead a long, long time — indistinguishable in death.

Charlotte decided it *did* matter, though. Those two years might mean nothing in the sweep of history, but they were important to the people who had lived them. It was all they had. Whether the time was filled with joy or sadness was irrelevant. They'd lived to experience it.

In the end, everyone, except for a very few, are forgotten, and Charlotte was starting way behind the eight ball. Seventeen years wasn't very much time to cement a legacy, especially if you'd lived her life. As this bleak calculus continued circling her brain, she looked down at her sleeve and realized the most horrible thing of all about being eternally young: she would be wearing the same clothes *forever*.

The superficiality of the thought reminded her of the Wendys, and her desire to be alive unnerved her like an e-mail from an ex-friend.

Charlotte kicked off her shoes as soon as she got into the apartment, trying to shake the *not-wanting-to-be-dead-anymore* feeling. Being home, however, didn't have the relaxing effect she had hoped it would. It was more than just her old life that was plaguing her now. After all she had done for the Dead Ed kids, all the personal changes she'd made, she wondered, why she still felt so excluded. So alone.

Maddy had it right, Charlotte surmised, even though she never came right out and said it. She was back to being second or even third fiddle. Now that they were through the looking glass or whatever, they didn't need her anymore. All she got from them now was busy signals. She knew they were tied up being reunited and all, and that the other girls especially did not approve of her friendship with Maddy, but who else did she have? Besides, Prue didn't like Scarlet either at first, as Charlotte recalled, and Pam thought nothing of shunning her over the whole Miss Wacksel episode. Maybe they were all

just showing their true colors now that they didn't need her anymore.

Charlotte crawled into her top bunk and continued feeling sorry for herself. Just then, Maddy walked in and looked as if she'd been rushing.

"Why didn't you tell me you were leaving?" she asked nervously. "We always walk home together."

"I didn't want to bother you."

"You're never a bother, Char," Maddy said endearingly. "Something on your mind?"

"Oh, nothing."

"You can tell me," Maddy urged.

Charlotte paused for a second and then decided she felt secure enough in their friendship to really open up.

"I miss . . . everything," Charlotte confided. "I feel different all of a sudden. I thought I was over it, over all of them, and totally changed in really profound ways, but now I think that was all just one big rationalization."

"How so?" Maddy asked, more like a therapist than a friend.

"I did what I was asked to do," Charlotte went on. "I made the hard choices Brain wanted me to."

"Brain?" Maddy asked.

"My Dead Ed teacher," Charlotte babbled, totally on a roll now. "I made every sacrifice for my *friends*," she blurted, "to get us all here."

"And for what? What did all that do-gooding get you?"

"I just thought, hoped, that, well, that things would really

be different for me here," Charlotte said quietly. "But it isn't. It's like this world is a Mac and I'm a PC."

"Heaven isn't all it's cracked up to be? Is that what you are trying to say?"

Charlotte hadn't really thought about it, but Maddy had a good point, once again. Charlotte had never really entertained the notion that *this* was *it*. Heaven couldn't be a phone bank, could it?

☙

Charlotte spent another day staring at the phone on her desk and trying to tune out the chatter from the other interns' calls. She couldn't even sneak away with the damn video camera constantly trained on her and Mr. Markov constantly walking by in the same pattern every few minutes like some kind of supernatural jail warden. Kim's calls were the most annoying and the most difficult to ignore.

Charlotte loved talking on the phone too: that wasn't the issue. It's just that Kim was so . . . sure of herself. So sure about what was right and what was wrong. Charlotte had felt that at the Fall Ball, right before they all crossed over. But she wasn't so sure what was right anymore. How can you be expected help anyone else if your own gray matter was one big gray muddle?

Charlotte struggled with these big ideas and covered her ears. This whole experience, she thought, was like being a mouse caught in a maze, except there was no cheese at the end to guide her through. She'd lost her life, her friends, her

future, and now maybe even her mind. She was trapped in a state of perpetual puberty and in the same outfit *forever,* and her payback for all this sacrifice? She got to help other people, or might get to, if her phone would ever, just once, ring!

She looked up at the lens of the camera and mouthed slowly:

"HELP ME."

Damen's legs were bouncing nervously as he sat silently in the still hospital room, positioned equidistant from Petula and Scarlet. For perhaps the first time in his life, he felt out of control, not just of the circumstances but of himself as well. He prided himself on being an athlete, after all, disciplined, determined, and optimistic. He was a winner in sports and in life and had the resume to prove it. He never considered losing, even when it was inevitable, such was his faith in himself and in the power of positive thinking. The dreary thoughts and increasing hopelessness of this situation, however, were new territory for him, mentally and emotionally. Mostly emotionally.

He could stand in the pocket and face down a core of blitzing linebackers without a second thought, but he couldn't face his own feelings. That's what made Petula so easy for him to date. No depth required. He could tote her around like one of his sports trophies, more a prize for others to envy than for him to value. But being with Scarlet had changed him, or at least it had begun to.

He began thinking about all the things he should have told Scarlet but didn't have the courage to say. Not so much about

stopping her from trying to cross over — she was too stubborn for that — but other things. Things like how much he cared for her, how much he missed her. How much he needed her. Things she needed to hear from him.

Desperate, he reached out to her the only way he knew how, through music. They had exchanged songs and albums like love letters from their earliest days together, and even if she couldn't hear him, she just might, he fantasized, be able to hear their music. He reached into his backpack and pulled out his iPod, loaded with bands she had turned him on to, most of them way cooler than anything he'd ever heard before. He gently pushed the speaker buds in each of her ears, and, recalling their first real date, scrolled to the track he was after — Artist>Death Cab For Cutie>Album>Plans>Song>*I Will Follow You into the Dark* — selected the song and hit play.

As the tinny sound bled from the headphones into the hospital room, the "if onlys" started swirling in his mind like a flock of diseased pigeons. Maybe he *had* made too much of Petula's illness, or maybe his expression or tone of voice revealed an unconscious flicker of dormant affection for Petula, despite his true feelings for Scarlet. Maybe that's what really set Scarlet off. But he was only trying to help Petula for Scarlet's sake. How could she not know that? Was bringing back Petula Scarlet's way of saving her sister *and* their troubled relationship?

Whatever Scarlet's motivation, he needed her to return. And for Scarlet to come back, Petula needed to also. However out of sync they were before, Scarlet and Damen were now on the same page. They both wanted Petula back.

Chapter 9

Bird on the Wire

If I, if I have been unkind,
I hope that you can just let it go by.
If I, if I have been untrue,
I hope you know it was never to you.
—Leonard Cohen

Live and learn, but really, Death is the best teacher.

—◆—

When you're faced with death you are forced to dig deep within yourself to understand who you really are and what you really feel. It rubs you raw, like a harsh facial peel, scrubbing away the mask of denial, excuses, and other gunk built up over a lifetime. What's left is not always so pretty to look at, at least not at first. Scarlet was hoping that her near-death experience wasn't going to become a life sentence.

 carlet had no idea where she might find Charlotte, but felt herself drawn, almost like a homing pigeon, back to Hawthorne High. Back to Dead Ed. Why, she could not imagine. Everyone was gone as far as she knew. Graduated. What was the point of turning up in an empty classroom? She was compelled nonetheless and followed her gut back to school.

For a second, she thought about Petula as she floated in the building and how odd it must have felt to come back to a familiar place, but with all the familiar faces gone. And of Charlotte too. How scary was it to be in a new place, to be the new kid?

As she hovered down the long hallway, her worst fears were confirmed. The school appeared to be vacant, but before she could be completely discouraged, she heard voices in the distance. She zeroed in on the sounds and, sure enough, saw a light emitting from the last classroom. She approached

it, stopping to eavesdrop just outside, and peered in the window.

"This must be it," Scarlet thought. "Dead Ed."

She looked through again, this time for a bit longer, hoping to spy Charlotte or anyone she recognized.

"Come in, come in, whoever you are," Ms. Pierce said playfully.

Scarlet reached down tentatively for the polished brass doorknob and, with some effort, turned it until the latch released and she could pull the heavy door open.

Ms. Pierce was a gentle woman of indeterminate age: pleasant-looking with a few wrinkles and a firm but caring voice. Her hair was tied up in a bun held there by a number two pencil, and she was wearing a smart silk long-sleeve blouse with a conservatively cut wool skirt. She seemed from an era when a person might as easily look fifty years old as thirty. A time, it occurred to Scarlet, now long passed. She felt badly about not having an apple to leave on Ms. Pierce's desk.

"Welcome. We've been expecting you, but . . . ," Ms. Pierce stammered. "I'm afraid I don't know your name, miss."

"Um, Scarlet, Scarlet Kensington, ma'am," she replied in an uncharacteristically respectful tone. "But I don't think you've been expecting *me*."

"Of course we have, *Scarlet*," Ms. Pierce assured her, emphasizing Scarlet's name so as to commit it to memory. "And there is your seat, the last open desk, at the back."

Scarlet had a feeling she knew where this was going, but before she could object, Ms. Pierce handed her a textbook, took her by the arm, and led her halfway to the seat. Scarlet

looked from side to side along the way and realized that there was not a soul in the room whom she recognized. This was not good. Rather than pipe up, however, Scarlet was determined to have a little patience and wait until class was over to approach Ms. Pierce with her dilemma. No point, she thought, in making the real dead kids feel like she was slumming it or something.

"Now class," Ms. Pierce resumed, "as we are all here together at last, let's review the orientation film one last time. You can follow along in your Deadiquette books."

The lights dimmed and Scarlet watched the film out of the corner of one eye and scanned her classmates with the other. She definitely did not recognize these kids. Then Scarlet was startled by a tap on her shoulder.

"Hi, Scarlet," a boy behind her said as she turned to look at him. "I'm Gary."

Gary, or Green Gary as he was known to his friends on the Other Side, was a nice, outdoorsy-looking kid dressed in baggy burlap clothes and hemp sneakers. He appeared totally normal except that his lower torso was misshapen and almost completely twisted around, like an old tree trunk.

"Hi, Gary," Scarlet whispered, trying hard to look him in the eye given his posture. "I'm looking for a girl named Charlotte Usher. Do you know her?"

"No," Gary answered quietly, "but I haven't been here as long as some of the others."

"Hey, Lisa," he whispered over to the next row. "Do you know some girl named Charlotte?"

Lipo Lisa was a totally groomed, moisturized, waxed, and buff girl. Even in the darkened classroom, she seemed to shine

and sparkle. The kind of girl who could give Petula and the Wendys a run for their money, Scarlet thought, except she wasn't a showhorse, she was a workhorse. Lisa was multitasking, watching the movie and doing book curls with her Deadiquette text, when Gary interrupted her workout.

"Never heard of her," Lisa grunted, barely breaking her rhythm.

"Thanks anyway," Scarlet said sarcastically. "Guess she's too busy working her jelly to say much, huh?"

"She *can't* say much," Gary said. "She died during a botched liposuction procedure on her neck and her facial muscles are pretty much paralyzed."

"She must have had her brain sucked out first," Scarlet quipped.

"Lisa considers herself the wave of the future, a beauty martyr," Gary said sincerely.

"Well, I hope she gets to meet the seventy-two plastic surgeons at some point, then," Scarlet cracked.

She began idly checking out whatever names on toe tags she could read in the dim glow of the projector. There was Polly, Tilly, Bianca, and Andy, to name a few. Scarlet was just starting to imagine how each of these kids died, but didn't need to, thanks to an unexpected whisper in her ear from Gary.

"There's A.D.D. Andy, a skater who tried to five-oh it off a cement truck," Gary informed her. "Only the cement churner turned on, and well, Andy was sidewalk."

"Jackass," Scarlet said devilishly.

"Yeah, he did get a lot of hits on YouTube though," Gary said, trying to be positive.

"And Tilly over there?" Scarlet asked.

"If the lights were up you wouldn't need to ask," Gary said with a smile. "Tanning Tilly got fried in a tanning bed. A world-class UV addict. Too greedy with the bulbs."

"That's hot," Scarlet mocked, her cutting sense of humor returning for the first time in a while. "She got a killer tan."

"That is Blogging Bianca," Gary said, pointing to a girl who had her fingers curved as if she was ready to type at any second. "Her blog was her life."

"Whose isn't?" Scarlet smirked, one of her pet peeves being the amount of valuable time people waste blogging and pushing mundane personal observations in their own little cyber sweatshops for mass consumption.

"Unfortunately, that's what it cost her," Gary explained. "She got a DVT, you know, a blood clot from not moving around enough. Too many snarky entries, too little stretching out."

"*Too* much information." Scarlet squirmed, pun totally intended. "Talk about logging out."

"What about you, Gary. How did you . . . get here?" Scarlet asked.

"Oh, I was driving my hybrid and I lost control. I swerved to save a tree, and instead, I plowed into the side of a Target."

"Bull's-eye," Scarlet said, stifling her giggle with her hand.

"Yeah, but the tree was unharmed, thank God," Gary said, still reveling in his success.

"You look older than the others," Scarlet said.

"Oh, actually, I'm the youngest here, I think," Gary said. "I probably look older because I only ate organic, no preservatives."

"Oh," Scarlet replied, trying not to look too shocked at the fact that Gary looked as old as her dad. "Bet you never got carded."

"No, and never will," Gary said with a momentary twinge of sadness in his voice.

"And *you*?" a mocking voice called to Scarlet from the other side of the room. "How did *you* get here?"

"Don't mind Paramour Polly," Gary said. "She's jealous of everyone. She died stealing her best friend's boyfriend. They were making out on the train tracks and . . ."

"I can figure out the rest, thanks," Scarlet said, cutting the conversation short. She had heard all she wanted or needed to.

After learning about her classmates, Scarlet directed her attention to the screen. The film continued with lessons from Billy and Butch on the proper use of "special abilities." Scarlet actually found it fascinating, but kept reminding herself she was only auditing this class. This stuff was all superfluous since she wasn't really dead.

The lights came up and Ms. Pierce dismissed everyone, but remained at her desk. Scarlet trailed the rest of the kids out of class and then stopped to talk with the teacher.

"Can I help you, Scarlet?" Ms. Pierce offered kindly.

"I hope so," Scarlet said with total seriousness. "You see, I don't belong here."

"We all feel that way at first, dear," Ms. Pierce. "You'll get used to it."

"I don't want to get used . . ." Scarlet stopped herself. "What I meant to say is, I'm not like the rest of you."

"What do you mean, Scarlet?" the teacher asked a bit curiously.

"I'm not dead, ma'am," Scarlet said. "Yet."

Ms. Pierce was a bit skeptical of what Scarlet was telling her, but glancing down at her roll sheet, she could not find Scarlet's name. She continued to listen, this time a bit more closely.

"Then why are you here?" Ms. Pierce said. "It is not exactly top of the list for teenagers."

"I'm looking for someone who *is* dead," Scarlet answered. "A girl named Charlotte Usher."

"I'm sorry, she's not in this class," Ms. Pierce advised, looking over her attendance roster once again. "Honestly, I have no idea how you would find her."

"I don't understand much about how all this stuff works, but I know that she graduated."

"Well, that's the problem, Miss Kensington," Ms. Pierce explained. "None of us here know where that is, but we are all waiting for an opportunity to be taken there."

The tone of Ms. Pierce's voice indicated to Scarlet that she had held out hope that the new student would be the one to lead them over.

"I'm sorry if I've created any confusion."

"You've created much more than confusion," Ms. Pierce said enigmatically. "Since there is nothing I can do for you now, why don't you take a spare room for the night at Hawthorne Manor and perhaps we can sort this out tomorrow."

"Thank you," Scarlet said, her voice cracking slightly from the strain.

Scarlet was getting really anxious about time, and what might

be going on at the hospital, but without any other options, she decided that it would be interesting to be at Hawthorne Manor again, as a guest rather than a waitress in the café.

❧

Scarlet arrived at Hawthorne Manor much like she would for work, but now she had special access to the actual dorm. It looked grand and beautiful, just as she remembered it had the first time. She walked in the huge wooden doors and through the marbled foyer, proud that she had helped to save such a place. No one was around, as far as she could tell.

She stepped toward the massive staircase and then up to the bedrooms, looking over her shoulder the whole way, alert to any uptight, resentful ghosts that might reside there these days. She noticed name plates on all the doors as she walked down the hall and then came to Charlotte's old room, which, as luck would have it, appeared to be unoccupied. It was strange for her to walk through the door, since last time, she'd pretty much floated in the huge stained-glass window.

She ran her finger along the fireplace mantel and thought about Charlotte and everything that had happened. She thought about Damen as well and wondered if he'd still be hovering over Petula in the hospital room, or if maybe he'd found a minute to tear up over her, stroke her hand, and call her back from the brink too. Unexpectedly, however, Scarlet found herself thinking mostly about Petula and how she could save her. Just then, she heard a rapping at the bedroom door.

"Scarlet?" a soft voice called out.

"Yeah . . . ?" Scarlet asked cautiously, hoping she wasn't so tired she was now hearing things . . . or worse.

It was Green Gary, with an unexpected invitation.

"Some of us are hanging out in the meeting room. You can join us if you want."

Scarlet was drained but thought this might be a good opportunity to get some info out of the kids.

"Sure," she said, opening the door and scooting through the hallway and down the stairs after him.

"What up, paleface?" Tilly asked, mocking Scarlet's porcelain skin, which appeared even more translucent in her ghostly state.

Ordinarily, Scarlet would have been offended, but looking at Tilly, who resembled one of those puckered, peeling radiation zombies from a cheapo old sci-fi flick, her rigorously sunblocked complexion did pale in comparison. Tilly totally redefined "hot mess" and Scarlet didn't feel the need to "burn" her any further.

"Can't we all just get along?" Green Gary asked, coming to Scarlet's defense.

"It's okay," Scarlet responded brusquely. "I'm not here to make friends."

Polly looked Scarlet over and felt threatened by her casual style and natural beauty, not to mention Green Gary's overattentiveness toward her.

"Well then, Tartlet," she chimed in cattily, "what are you doing here?"

"Yes," Blogging Bianca inquired, her hands poised over an

imaginary keyboard like a bloggerazzi. "What is your pur-
pose here?"

It was strangely surreal how Bianca froze after each
statement, as if she were on a real-life vlog. The only thing
missing was the "play again" arrow over her face.

"I'm looking for someone, actually two people," Scarlet
said softly. "And I don't know how to find them."

"Friends or family?" Bianca asked.

"Both," Scarlet answered.

"Can't be both. Friends are people you choose to be around
and family are people you have to be around," Bianca said,
spinning the idea into a potential blog entry, but then realizing that she needed to at least try to be helpful. "I can
post an alert," she said semi-sincerely, overlooking the fact
that everyone she could possibly alert was already in the
room.

"What, no milk carton, dumbass?" Andy shouted at Bianca
as he worked out some new freestyle tricks on his skateboard.
"She needs to actually *do* something, like look for these girls."

"I'm hoping the friend can lead me to the family," Scarlet
said. "And I'm running out of time."

"I see," Gary said. "Everybody is just a little disappointed.
We were kind of hoping you were here for us."

Scarlet looked around and saw sadness, frustration, loneliness, but not anger.

"I guess we all are waiting for someone to come and save
us," Scarlet concluded.

Scarlet settled under the heavy sheets of the comfy four-poster and had barely drifted off to sleep when her eyes opened again, forced by the moonlight that crept, like a false dawn, up the colored window pane. Her troubled conscience wasn't helping much either, now totally immune to her Chinese sleeping chants.

The possibility of catching any shut-eye was looking more and more remote now, so she picked up right where she left off, obsessing about her rash decision. Wouldn't she have been much more help at the hospital than she was trolling around between worlds? And what about all the anxiety she must be causing her mom? Damen? As she turned her face away from the moon's icy glare, she noticed Charlotte's old Deadiquette book sitting on the nightstand next to the bed.

Charlotte's text, she remembered, was different than the rest. Older, if she recalled correctly. She pulled the book she'd been given from under the blanket and began thumbing through each, comparing pages and chapters. She came across the chapter on possession in Charlotte's book, which was missing from hers.

"Been there, done, that," Scarlet said, flipping right by the ritual.

She turned all the way to the end of each book, matching page for page, but it seemed the possession stuff was the only difference. Until she got to the very last page. In Charlotte's book, there was one extra. It looked more like an order form or an application than actual text. Easy to overlook, unless you were specifically looking for it.

The heading on the page read: EARLY DECISION.

Chapter 10

This Is How I Disappear

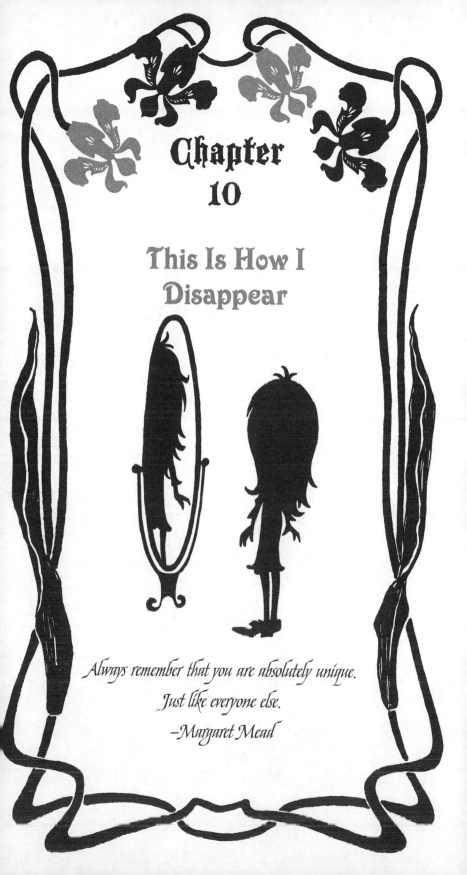

Always remember that you are absolutely unique.
Just like everyone else.
–Margaret Mead

Timing is everything.

We let some people in and keep others out for all kinds of reasons, most of them having to do with timing. The difference between good timing and bad timing, between making friends or making problems, is usually just a matter of readiness. Dead, alive, or in-between, nothing is more futile than being in the right place at the wrong time.

etula and Virginia both had taken seats on the bench but were not saying much. Petula noticed the girl looking down at her feet and made a preemptive comment.

"*They* took my polish off," Petula said, pointing out the obvious hatchet job so that the little girl wouldn't have a chance to point it out first.

"So?" Virginia said in her best who-cares tone of voice.

"Well, you can't go around with ratty-looking feet," Petula admonished. "If you don't care about yourself, who's going to care about you?"

"Aren't there more important things to worry about?" Virginia asked.

She looked at Petula, some dark roots poking out from under her blond, frazzled hair extensions, and realized that there probably wasn't anything more important to Petula.

"Don't kid yourself," Petula seethed. "When you look good, like I do, you make everyone else around you look good. Beauty matters."

"I know all about it," Virginia said a little wearily.

"Oh, really?" Petula spit back condescendingly.

"Yes, really," Virginia insisted, mocking Petula's grating voice.

The girls glared at each other, facing off.

"I don't need a lesson from you about the importance of beauty," Virginia responded. "You know that picture you get in the frame, the one of the little girl with the perfect face and smile, the one that makes you want to buy the frame?"

"Yeah," Petula said. "Actually my sister used to keep those pictures in and pretend that she had another sister, not me."

"Well, that *was* me," Virginia said. "From there I went on to be one of the most winning pageant girls around."

"Oh, that's nice," Petula sniffed. "I never really had time for that kind of stuff. I was always too busy with my friends, you know, having a social life."

Petula tried to play it off, but she knew she'd been trumped. She'd secretly wanted to be one of those pageant girls. It really suited her competitive personality, she thought, but her mom felt otherwise. Petula always thought it was some conspiracy Scarlet and her mom came up with to keep her from ever fully realizing her outer swan.

"You have friends?" Virginia asked with a mix of sarcasm and curiosity.

"I have two *best* friends, in fact," Petula said, rubbing it in.

"How good for you," Virginia responded, a little more wistfully this time.

Both girls had taken measure of each other, and after round one they returned to their "corners," each with a bit more respect for the other. They had more in common than Petula would have expected and more than Virginia preferred to think.

"I take it you never won a Miss Congeniality title," Petula said after a while, smiling at the tweenager.

"Actually, I don't even know what I won," Virginia answered indifferently. "I couldn't care less anyway."

"Oh, you care," Petula said with a smirk. "I'm sure you could have quit any time you wanted."

Virginia remained silent.

"But you didn't," Petula pressed, "did you?"

Petula accepted Virginia's awkward silence as enough of an answer and turned her focus back where it belonged, on herself, especially her pedicure.

"Look, they didn't even take it off the whole way," Petula said, clearly distressed. "I'm never going to find nail polish remover . . . here."

After a few seconds, Virginia came through with practical advice.

"You just need to soak your feet in some warm water, peel off the excess polish, and then soak your nails in some lemon juice for naturally white tips," Virginia offered, easing Petula's concerns.

"How did you know that?" Petula said in amazement.

"I know lots of stuff," Virginia said mockingly. "Lots of mindless, unimportant stuff . . ."

"I think there's a lot we can learn from each other," Petula said with a gleam spearing off of her colored contact lens. "You're going to be the little sister I always wanted!"

With that cold remark, the temperature in the room suddenly plummeted. Both girls tried to hide the unspoken fears that had been lurking under their conversation and slid closer together, each pulling her hospital gown down as far as it would stretch, which was not nearly far enough.

"Damn cotton!" Petula cursed, hunching over slightly. "It has no give."

❧

Dr. Kaufman, a hot young neurology resident who magically transformed Hawthorne Hospital into *General Hospital,* came into the room to examine both Kensington girls as Damen kept vigil between them. The doctor started with Petula, examining her as thoroughly as Dr. Patrick and the nurses before had.

Damen laughed a little to himself at the sight of the doctor running his hands along Petula's arms and legs, checking her skin for rashes. This is the kind of guy she'd really go for, he thought, and was instantly hit by a wave of sadness, realizing she might never have the chance.

The doctor examined Scarlet as well, and Damen felt a twinge of jealousy as he watched Kaufman handle her, performing the required neurological and motor testing. Damen couldn't help but think that he'd rather be "playing doctor" with Scarlet than watching the real thing. Kaufman held her lids open, shined his penlight in Scarlet's eyes, and noted his findings on the ever-present clipboards hanging from each bed.

For Damen, these three-times-a-day examinations were almost like online updates tracking the arrival of a plane that had been delayed due to bad weather. If there was any improvement in either girls' condition, it might mean that Scarlet had been successful, that she was closer to returning to him and closer to living than dying.

"So, what's the verdict?" Damen said anxiously, pushing for a concrete answer to ease his mind.

"I'm going to be frank with you," Dr. Kaufman said.

"Please," Damen replied, picking up Scarlet's hand and holding it tightly.

"I'm afraid their vitals aren't as strong as they were yesterday," Dr. Kaufman said. "And the neurological evaluation is unchanged."

"What does that mean?" Damen asked naively, knowing damn well what it meant but not wanting to face it.

"It appears that both of their conditions are deteriorating," Dr. Kaufman said cryptically as he initialed the exam sheet, turned, and left the room.

Damen hung his head over Scarlet and then thought of a million questions he wanted to ask, if only to feel like he was actually doing something. He bolted out of the room after Dr. Kaufman, and saw him dip into another patient's room at the end of the hall.

He stopped short of the doorway when he heard soft whimpering coming from inside the room. He peeked in and spied Dr. Kaufman beginning a new exam. Then he saw an agonized couple, hovering hopefully over a beautiful young girl, not more than twelve years old, who appeared to be desperately ill. Damen may not have been a doctor, but he could tell she was in trouble. He felt himself on the verge of tears — for the little girl, for Scarlet, or for himself, he could not be sure.

Life's not fair, Damen realized for the first time in his super-popular, super-connected, super-successful existence as he turned and walked back to Petula and Scarlet's room.

Scarlet raised her hand just as Ms. Pierce was about to begin her lecture for the day.

"Yes, Scarlet," the teacher said, acknowledging her.

"I was up late reading my Deadiquette book last night and I understand all of it, except for one thing," Scarlet explained.

"What's that?" Ms. Pierce asked.

"Can you please tell me about 'Early Decision'?" Scarlet requested, preparing for a negative reaction of some sort from the usually genial school marm.

Ms. Pierce's expression hardened slightly, and she seemed at a loss for words momentarily.

"Early Decision?" she muttered, clearly taken aback. "I'm not sure what you mean."

Tilly, Gary, Bianca, and the rest all looked over at Scarlet with bemused looks on their faces, curious about the fact that the new girl had been able to stump Ms. Pierce, who until now seemed to them to be all-knowing.

"It was in an old Deadiquette book in my room," Scarlet explained. "The very last page."

Scarlet held up the application from the back of the room for Ms. Pierce and the whole class to see.

"I know what it means," Polly called out, breaking the silence and putting her two cents in. "It's when you decide to leave a party before your boyfriend's real girlfriend gets there."

Polly's analysis sounded a little more biographical than anyone cared to hear and was instantly dismissed by the other students.

"I think it's when you have to decide if you're gonna do a lip trick off a shark tank at the zoo," Andy interjected, bringing his own daredevil perspective to the discussion.

"You are both right," Ms. Pierce said surprisingly. "In a metaphorical way, of course."

"Huh?" Scarlet said, voicing what the rest of the class was already thinking.

"Early Decision is a process by which a single student may bypass Dead Ed," Ms. Pierce explained carefully.

"Oh, is that all?" Tilly asked, her famously impatient personality burning brightly like the harsh UV rays that killed her. "You mean I've been waiting around here for nothing?"

"It is not something we teach, Tilly," Ms. Pierce answered firmly. "Because it is dangerous for the applicant as well as the rest of the class."

Scarlet tried to get things back on track.

"You said Polly and Andy were both sorta right?" Scarlet asked.

"It is about leaving for the Other Side before one is deemed ready," Ms. Pierce went on, somewhat vaguely, "negotiating the biggest obstacle of all."

Nothing could be worse than where she was right now, and besides, was anyone every *really* ready, Scarlet thought.

"Why is it so dangerous?" Scarlet asked naively. "Everyone here, well, almost everyone, is already dead."

"You do reveal yourself, Scarlet," Ms. Pierce said. "There are things worse than death, but not truly being one of us, you cannot yet fully appreciate what I am trying to say."

"I'm listening," Scarlet said.

"You are taking up a seat meant for someone else," Ms. Pierce explained, getting right to the point.

"Okay," Scarlet muttered, insulted by the demure teacher's

directness. It wasn't the first time she'd been accused of taking up space, but this was different.

"But leaving may be worse than staying," Ms. Pierce went on.

"Not for me," Scarlet quipped, her choice seeming perfectly clear.

"Don't be too sure," Ms. Pierce continued, a stern tone in her voice. "By coming here, you have placed us all in jeopardy. You've made your problem *our* problem."

Scarlet looked around the room and saw the anxiety on all the kids' faces.

"I was only trying to save my sister."

"That is admirable," Ms. Pierce said sympathetically, her voice softening. "But there are often unintended consequences of even the most noble actions."

"I understand that now" was all the response Scarlet could muster.

"I'm not sure you do," the teacher advised. "If you *are* accepted early, there is no telling where you will wind up. Conversely, if your application is rejected . . ."

"Yes?" Scarlet asked, hanging on her answer.

"We only get one chance to cross over, Scarlet," Ms. Pierce informed. "Each of us alone, or all of us together. Dead Ed exists because the odds of success are greater if the attempt is made as a group, a more prepared group. We take great pains to bring everyone along, make sure they've learned the right lessons from their lives and their deaths."

"You're losing me," Scarlet pleaded, her head spinning.

"Simply put, if you fail, we all pay," Ms. Pierce advised.

"You may not be the One to help us, but you could very easily be the one to damn us. And yourself."

"I won't fail," Scarlet said. "I can't."

"I can submit this for you, Scarlet," Ms. Pierce said quietly, "but you must realize that there is no guarantee."

"I'm willing to take the risk," Scarlet said, presenting the application tentatively, her hand shaking. "I need to try to make everything right again."

Scarlet turned to face the class. It was their souls she was gambling with too, after all, and she felt she owed them an acknowledgment, if not an explanation.

"I hope you understand," she said, polling their expressions for her answer. "I have to try."

"Are you sure you want to do this?" A.D.D. Andy asked, questioning an action for the first time.

"Have faith." Scarlet smiled at him, as all the kids behind her crossed their fingers.

The teacher folded the application neatly in thirds and walked over to a brass plaque on the wall. There was a slit in the faceplate, not unlike the mail slot in an old farmhouse door. Ms. Pierce stood there for a second, then placed the paper half in, half out, waiting for Scarlet's consent to nudge it into eternity.

Scarlet exhaled confidently, reassuring herself and preparing for what, exactly, she did not know.

Ms. Pierce slid the application gracefully through the slot, and before she could turn back to Scarlet, Scarlet was gone.

Chapter 11

She Sells Sanctuary

I'll pick up the pieces
I'll carry on somehow
Tape the broken parts together
And limp this love around
—PJ Harvey

We are all rubberneckers in Life.

Minding other people's business, transforming their problems into entertainment for ourselves and basically cheating them out of their own tragedies. We devour horrible and intimate details ravenously like baby birds at feeding time, only rarely connecting the unfortunate dots that bring the bigger, sadder picture into view.

addy walked into the break room
and right by the other interns without saying
a word, as usual. It wasn't just that she didn't
interact with anyone besides Charlotte, it was that she literally
ignored them. Even worse, Charlotte was beginning to treat
them the same way.

"What the hell is she doing here anyway," CoCo prodded.

"Yeah," Violet gabbed. "Why wasn't she in Dead Ed with
us? Does anyone even know the first thing about her?"

In fact, nobody did. Even Charlotte, who'd been so obsessed with herself, or busy answering Maddy's questions,
that she'd never even thought to ask how or why Maddy was
there. The girls were in mid-gossip when she walked in.

"Speak of the devil," Prue said, turning her head to Maddy.

The other girls giggled and continued their conversation.

"Is there a problem?" Maddy asked firmly, silencing them.

"Yes," Pam said just as sternly. "You. Charlotte was happy when she got here."

"And then what happened?" Maddy interrupted brusquely. "You all had your happy endings and no time for her. If not for me, she'd have no one."

"Charlotte is in a vulnerable state," Kim added rationally, with a bit less venom than the others. "A real friend would not take her calls, isolate her, and feed her doubts and fears."

"And by real friends, you are referring to . . . ?" Maddy let the question trail off and burrow into the guilty consciences of the rest of the interns around the table.

It was true they hadn't made much time for Charlotte since crossing over. Between their new "lives" and work, it was getting harder and harder to spend quality time together. But after all of them had been through so much together, Charlotte had to know how much they cared.

Pam took particular offense to Maddy's suggestion, considering she'd known Charlotte longer than anyone, even Scarlet.

"I don't need any lectures about being a friend to Charlotte from some latecomer like you," Pam argued. "We are doing what we need to do, what we were assigned to do."

"So am I," Maddy responded vaguely, and split, abruptly leaving the interns, and the matter, hanging.

֍

Scarlet looked around and saw that she was someplace else. Where, exactly, she had no idea. It appeared to be a slightly dreary gated community — fenced in, with paved sidewalks,

and a boot camp vibe. In the distance, she could see a stick-thin single residential tower. It was getting dark, so she headed for the apartment building, the nearest sign of light, if not life, hoping to get some information about Charlotte.

She walked in the entranceway and was stopped by the doorman.

"I'm looking for someone," Scarlet said nervously.

The man looked her up and down and then noticed her "Damned" T-shirt. Damen had brought it to the hospital for her to wear on her "little trip."

"It's a band," she clarified, thinking this was not a good time or place to take any chances.

"Who are you looking for?" he replied tersely.

"Charlotte Usher?" she said sheepishly, half-expecting to get blanked by the doorkeep.

He looked up at the video camera scanning the entrance-way as if for an answer, and the red light blinked once.

"Seventeen," he said, and gestured toward the elevator.

Scarlet was in shock for a minute, frozen in place, not sure whether to run out the door or jump on the doorman and kiss him. She was going to see her best friend. Finally she could really have hope, not just faith, that her journey was worthwhile. Seventeen floors straight up might be the answer to her prayers and Petula's and her Mom's and probably Damen's too . . . or, she paused reflectively, the beginning of a nightmare.

She suddenly realized that she had no idea where she was or who this doorman guy was. Maybe this had all been a little too easy. Ms. Pierce warned there were no guarantees with

Early Decision, didn't she? Maybe her destiny was not to save Petula or herself — maybe it was to become a snack for some gigantic, seventeen-story evil reality show judge?

Scarlet turned to the doorman again and looked him over, trying to assess his character. He appeared imposing, but not dishonest. She decided he was basically a good soul and not likely to deceive her. And seventeen was "up" after all. The odds, she calculated, were in her favor. Whether she was just looking for an excuse to or not, she dismissed her doubts and went with her gut.

☙

Damen flipped through his magazine, glancing up at Scarlet and Petula at regular intervals. He watched the monitors, ready to alert the nurses or the doctors of any changes, good or bad, before any alarms sounded. Thankfully, he thought, both girls had remained stable for the past day or so, with no emergency intervention necessary. This was a relief to him and to Kiki Kensington, whom he'd called to reassure every few hours.

He rubbed the uncharacteristic stubble sprouting on his face, put the mag down, and reached for Scarlet's hand, which was hanging through the bedrail. He stroked her forearm and squeezed her fingers, trying his best to elicit some sort of reaction, even if it was just reflexive. And then he stopped caring whether he would get a response or not and just stroked her, lost in his thoughts of her. He was the only one in the world who really knew her. He knew that her favorite holiday was Daylight Saving Time, her favorite band changed based

on who could perform best live, and that her ideal day was hanging out in used bookstores, buying vintage jewelry, eating a burger at a greasy spoon and then catching an indie film in an art nouveau theater.

He stopped himself from remembering her as if she wasn't coming back, and instead began to wonder if there was some way he could help. He stared tenderly at Scarlet's face and could have sworn he saw the faintest trace of a smile cross her lips.

৩১৩

"Come in!" Charlotte yelled as she heard a light rap on the door. It was virtually impossible to hear, but oddly Charlotte did. She'd yet to have a visitor, and the prospect of maybe Pam, Prue, DJ, Jerry, or any of her friends stopping by was exciting.

As the door slowly opened, a hand could be seen reaching in. The hand was pale and the nails were adorned in super-dark nail polish. She knew those digits like they were her own. Charlotte could not speak.

"What? What is it?" Maddy asked, never having seen Charlotte at a loss for words before.

"Is it the Grim Reaper?" Charlotte managed to dribble out of her mouth in the direction of the door, completely perplexing Maddy.

The door creaked open a little farther, and the hand reached in even more.

"No, not a vampire either," Scarlet said, flinging the door wide open.

Charlotte stood there, paralyzed and mute from the vision

before her. She could not believe her eyes, or more like her heart wouldn't let her believe her eyes.

"Scarlet!"

"Charlotte!"

Without another word, the two walked toward one another, stared into each other's eyes, and embraced. It was like they were attempting possession again, only this time, they were holding on to one another for dear life.

"I missed you," Scarlet said, squeezing hard.

"You have no idea," Charlotte said, barely able to get a hand free from Scarlet's bear hug to brush the familiar poker-straight black bangs out of Scarlet's face.

"You haven't changed a bit."

"No, I haven't," Charlotte said, a hint of melancholy in her voice. "I just can't believe you're here."

Charlotte wanted to jump up and down on her bed like a schoolgirl, but resisted for Scarlet's sake, and because Maddy was watching.

"Me either," Scarlet said, replaying in her head all the long-shot decisions that had brought her there.

The girls stood staring for a while longer, looking each other over again and again, not judgmentally, like the Wendys or Petula might, but with a genuine affection that was way beyond words. As they hugged one last time, Charlotte was suddenly startled. Something was missing. Scarlet's heartbeat. Charlotte couldn't feel it. The sign of life that always beckoned Charlotte each time they performed the ritual was gone.

"Why, I mean, how are you here?" she stammered, barely getting up the nerve to ask.

The smile left Scarlet's face and her eyes assumed a faraway look. Scarlet glanced at Charlotte and then at Maddy, seeking Charlotte's approval to talk freely in front of a stranger.

"I'm Maddy," Matilda said, extending her hand to make an introduction. "You must be Scarlet."

Scarlet reached out her hand wanly. There was something about her voice, like she'd heard it before, but Scarlet couldn't quite place it.

"It's okay," Charlotte said, sensing Scarlet's apprehension. "Maddy is my roommate."

"We're friends too," Maddy added, a bit too eagerly for Scarlet's taste.

"She just knows about you because I talk about you," Charlotte added, trying to defuse the awkwardness.

"Don't worry, it's all good stuff," Maddy laughed nervously, leaving Scarlet to wonder why it wouldn't be.

Charlotte noticed the stunned expression on Maddy's face. She seemed more worried than threatened by Scarlet's arrival.

"So this is paradise, huh?" Scarlet said, brushing by Maddy and taking in Charlotte's new dwelling. She walked toward the large windows that looked out on the cement esplanade and the semi-circular tract of generic, condo-like structures below. It all appeared even more Iron Curtain-ish to her from a bird's-eye view than from ground level. If this dreary, commonplace locale is "Up," Scarlet thought, what must it be like where Petula was surely headed.

"Scarlet?" Charlotte asked, fearing that Scarlet might have come to some harm, "Are you . . . ?"

"I'm here voluntarily," Scarlet replied.

Charlotte was momentarily relieved to hear that but totally confused by it.

"Suicide, huh?" Maddy said out of the side of her mouth, looking Scarlet's outfit up and down.

From the looks on their faces, Maddy could tell neither Charlotte or Scarlet was amused by her one-liners. She decided she better chill and listen rather than force a threesome prematurely.

"I'm not *dead*," Scarlet said, mentally shooting invisible pins into Maddy like some supernatural voodoo doll. "At least not yet, I hope."

"Then, why?" The danger Scarlet had likely put herself in was just beginning to dawn on Charlotte.

"To find you," Scarlet confessed. "You're the only one who can help me."

Charlotte was growing increasingly uneasy now as she began to think the worst. What could be so bad that only she — a long-dead teenager, a restless spirit with an uncertain past, present, and future of her own — could make a difference?

"Is it Damen?" Charlotte asked, not sure if she really wanted the answer.

Even after all this time, he was the first person who popped into her mind. She had to give him up, but had never completely given up on the idea of him.

"No," Scarlet said, noting the wistfulness in Charlotte's eyes. "It's Petula," she replied, letting the grim reality escape her lips for the first time. "She's . . . dying."

Scarlet's words tumbled over Charlotte like loose bricks

from a tall building. In life, Petula had been Charlotte's hero, and heroes are supposed to be invincible. Charlotte had been unlucky her whole life, and her own Fate, sad as it was, was just a part of that losing streak. Petula, on the other hand, Charlotte thought, was a winner, and nothing bad ever happened to winners. Despite her worry over Petula's plight, however, Charlotte found herself even more concerned about Scarlet's decision to cross over.

"How did you get here?" Charlotte asked clinically, far more calmly than she was feeling.

"I did the spell on my own," Scarlet began, "recalling our first time, recalling you . . ."

It suddenly dawned on Charlotte that her recent feelings of wanting to go back again and being dissatisfied with her new so-called-life might have been a side effect of Scarlet channeling her. The memory should have been a sweet one for Charlotte, but she became panicked instead.

"If you are here," Charlotte began, "where's the *rest* of you?"

"In the hospital," Scarlet answered sheepishly, "I guess?"

"You guess?"

"Damen tried to stop me," Scarlet explained, "but you know how I am."

Charlotte did indeed know how she was. She could easily picture Damen making his case and Scarlet ignoring him completely. In a flash, however, her anger passed and she found herself deeply touched by Scarlet's willingness to risk her own life to save her sister, given their rocky relationship, and was suddenly deeply committed to saving them both.

Chapter 12

Die Young, Stay Pretty

Once you're dead, you're made for life.
—Jimi Hendrix

Only the good die young.

———◆———

Whenever students meet their untimely demise in a horrible accident, from a random act of violence or a rare untreatable disease, they are instantly elevated by teachers, friends, and family into prized pupils, filled with promise— whether they actually were or not. They aren't remembered as a busload of mediocre students who perished in a crash, but are magically transformed instead into upstanding honor roll students in death. We need lost lives to have *meaning*. It's a comforting delusion, really. Like dead-spin. Unfortunately, you aren't around to appreciate it.

**S**tuck in the discharge office, Petula and Virginia were getting to know each other, for better or worse.

"Getting older isn't a bad thing," Virginia leaned in and whispered.

"It's not a good thing either," Petula said, turning up her nose as if her dog had pooped in the kitchen. "Everything sags and shrivels."

"A lot of people would feel lucky to grow older," Virginia said, almost somberly. "It's a gift."

Petula stared right through Virginia, seething at the naiveté of the little know-it-all, but then considered that maybe she had stumbled upon a real teaching moment in her life. With the Wendys and other girls at school, she was more of an icon, a role model. She led by example. And Scarlet, well, she would never get through to her. But here was an opportunity to

impart her wisdom, to imprint her philosophy on a whole new generation in her own unique way, with this little Virginia person as her messenger.

"No, it's tragic. Youth is a gift," Petula countered, admiring her own poppin' fresh bod. "Just ask any old person."

"That's pretty narrow-minded," Virginia fired back, showing surprising maturity. "What about wisdom?"

"I'd rather be hot than wise any day," Petula said. "I don't want to be one of those people who look back on the days when they were younger as their glory days."

"Not everyone is so unhappy with themselves," Virginia answered. "You are just projecting."

"You don't need to believe me," Petula sniffed dismissively. "Just check out any supermarket tabloid survey."

Petula consumed these things obsessively, not because she cared what others actually thought, but because they tended to reveal insecurities in them, weaknesses she could exploit.

"I've heard about some polls too," Virginia responded. "Like the one where people were asked what they would do differently if they only had a few months to live."

"And?" Petula asked, more curious than she was showing.

"Nothing," Virginia said. "Most people wouldn't change a thing. No Fifth Avenue shopping sprees, no cruises around the world, and no plastic surgery."

"Not surprising," Petula said coolly.

Virginia looked surprised and thought maybe she'd broken through just a little.

"There would be no point," Petula instructed. "The swelling would barely be down in six months."

Exasperation could barely describe Virginia's mood, though she was beginning to admire Petula's consistency.

"What about just changing who you are?" Virginia plied, taking one last shot at her argument. "On the inside."

"The best way to change who you are," Petula answered definitively, "is Photoshop."

"You're totally gonna be one of those wannabeens who roam around the mall trying to fit into child-size clothes with the logo of your favorite store sprawled across your middle-aged ass," Virginia said with unwavering confidence.

Petula's face went into screensaver mode to protect her from the harsh reality of the future she was picturing. She shook it off and re-engaged.

"Have you ever seen old-people feet?" Petula queried, offering up a striking visual. "Is that something you are looking forward to?"

"You should talk," Virginia came back, glancing down at Petula's big toe and botched pedicure.

"All I'm saying," Petula emphasized, "is that nobody goes looking for the Fountain of Old."

"If you base your whole life on looks, then I guess you're right," Virginia said snidely. "But I don't know if I'm ready for a whole generation of grandmas with the greatest boobs ever."

"Everyone bases their life on looks," Petula replied. "Either you have and use them to get somewhere or you make a lot of money so you can surround yourself with beautiful people. No one wants to be ugly or old. Life is a runway."

"Tell me about it," Virginia mumbled.

"People would rather be envied than respected," Petula

ranted. "They want attention, for any reason, good or bad, and they'll do anything to get it."

"Or live through anyone to get it," Virginia said cryptically.

"Oh, please, don't play victim and blame your life on your evil stage Mommy," Petula shot back unsympathetically. "That whole game is like a false pregnancy reading on a generic EPT!"

"Huh?" Virginia said, having no idea what Petula was talking about.

"When you first get the positive result, you're upset and crying to all your friends," Petula explained more clearly. "Then you test it again and it's negative. You're all relieved, but you secretly feel kind of down."

"Don't be shy," Virginia said sarcastically.

"You look down on the whole pageant thing because you were pushed into it and you're so over it now, and blah, friggin' blah," Petula continued, wrapping things up. "But once you were entered, the audience started to applaud, and you wanted to win, right?"

"Of course, everyone would rather win. We're conditioned that way," Virginia said. "It's all about the reward."

"And what were you being rewarded for?" Petula asked, interrupting. "Your looks. Your youth."

"That sucks."

"That's life," Petula summed up. "You've got to face the world as it is, not cling to the way you wish it was. Sometimes, Virginia," she lectured, "you just have to let go."

"Well, I still think old age is a gift," Virginia said, refusing to back down.

"Yeah, well, that's a gift that I hope comes with an exchange policy," Petula quipped.

All this bickering had killed a lot of time and kept Petula and Virginia from noticing that even as their argument heated up, the room had gotten colder. Both girls felt more and more afraid but were too proud to say what they were really thinking. Something wasn't right. Not right at all.

❧

The two best friends had barely stopped talking since Scarlet arrived and were lying curled up in Charlotte's top bunk, sleepover style, chitchatting and waiting for the morning to come. Maddy covered her head with a pillow but still couldn't block out the bull session entirely.

"I can't believe what you went through to get here," Charlotte marveled.

"I guess you could say I was *dying* to see you," Scarlet punned, black humor being her favorite kind.

"You were in Dead Ed?"

"Yes, but it was a totally different class, with different kids and a different teacher," Scarlet explained. "Nobody knew you."

"They didn't?" Charlotte asked, a little hurt.

"But I told them all about you."

She smiled at Charlotte, knowing that's what she secretly wanted to hear, and Charlotte smiled back at the fact that Scarlet knew that.

"The kids were really nice to me. I felt really badly dragging them into all this," Scarlet confided.

"Apparently not badly enough," Maddy interjected.

"But I couldn't stay, obviously," Scarlet continued, ignoring the heckling from the bunk below. "I was so afraid I was gonna get stuck there."

"Translation," Maddy interjected, "they kicked you out like a party crasher."

"No," Scarlet said. "I applied for Early Decision, and here I am."

"Crafty," Charlotte said, praising Scarlet's spirit-world savvy.

"*You* got accepted?" Maddy asked enviously.

"Yes," Scarlet said proudly, "I'm a graduate, just like you guys, except I'm not dead or anything."

"And all I got was this lousy T-shirt," Maddy mumbled.

Charlotte decided to ease the tension a little and redirected the conversation back to less controversial territory.

"What about Hawthorne?" Charlotte asked hesitantly. "Do they remember me there?"

Charlotte had that queasy feeling you get in your stomach on roller coasters. She was sure she'd be remembered, at least for a semester or something. But she prepared to hear the details of her irrelevance.

"It was weird for a while," Scarlet explained. "Nobody wanted to admit it had really happened."

"Better a has-been," Charlotte interjected, "than a wannabe."

"But then," Scarlet paused for effect, "they put your obituary in the center of the glass case in the lobby, next to all the other distinguished alumni, class presidents, former Homecoming queens, All-State jocks, Science Fair geeks, and other loathsome creatures."

"Coming from you," Charlotte giggled, "I'll take that as a compliment."

Charlotte was nearly bursting at her posthumous celebrity as Scarlet went on and on about how people who never even knew her were telling her story in the most warm and familiar terms. How, in the weeks following her passing, people would break out into spontaneous group hugs in the hallways and comfort one another — like they had to survive this tragedy together. As if they never knew that someone could die before this event, which showed them that they too were mortal. There were black ribbons handed out and grief counselors hired to help the student body through mourning someone they'd never even acknowledged. She had given them all something to be part of.

"Someone even found a hot roll on their school lunch tray that they said had an image of your face in it," Scarlet laughed. "It made the school paper."

This all should have been really uplifting for Charlotte, but rather than simply enjoying the celebration of her memory, she began to feel sad and a little bit cheated. Charlotte found herself wishing she could have been there to see it.

As their laughter subsided, a strange sadness came over Scarlet, too. She became fixated on that obituary she'd written for Charlotte and how close she and Petula might soon be to needing ones of their own. A double funeral was an increasing possibility. It was all getting more and more absurd, but less and less funny.

"This is the first time we've ever been together in *your*

room," Scarlet noted wistfully, feeling much closer to death than ever before.

"*Our* room," Maddy corrected pointedly.

"Don't worry," Charlotte reassured with a smile. "You are just visiting."

Scarlet loved Charlotte's ability to put a good face on anything. She believed Charlotte and believed *in* her, same as always. She had to. Despite Maddy's annoying presence, being with Charlotte took her back to a time when she was secure and everything was new and exciting. Now it was time to put that faith to the test.

"Damen is sitting in that room, waiting," Scarlet said anxiously. "Waiting for her . . . for me, to come back."

"Then you better get going," Maddy hinted.

"Scarlet, is all this really because of Petula?" Charlotte asked. "Or Damen?"

"No, well, I don't know, maybe," Scarlet fudged, not really knowing the answer herself. "He hasn't been home much since he started school, and now all of a sudden, when Petula is so sick, he pops up."

"It does make you wonder," Maddy intervened.

"He says it's because he wanted to take me to Homecoming," Scarlet explained, a bit defensively.

"Homecoming?" Charlotte mused aloud, trying hard to keep her mind from slipping into all the old delusions once again.

"We just haven't been connecting like we used to," Scarlet complained, seeming more vulnerable to Charlotte than she had before. "It's like we're in different worlds."

Charlotte knew all about being in different worlds, first-hand. She couldn't help but think that maybe it truly was she whom Damen had fallen for, but she immediately felt guilty for even letting the thought cross her mind. Maddy stayed quiet, gathering information and listening carefully to both girls spill their guts.

"Does he call you?" Charlotte asked curiously.

"Yes, he does, but it's not enough, you know?"

"Does he know how you feel?"

"No. And I don't really know how he feels," Scarlet said, clearly frustrated.

"Love is a battlefield," Maddy butted in, unable to restrain herself.

Damen's sympathy for Petula was really irksome to Scarlet, and the fact that they were experiencing a growing communication breakdown was making him much harder to read. Scarlet wanted to believe her main reason for seeking Charlotte was to help Petula, not something she was especially anxious to admit, but Charlotte was on to something. Restoring Petula, saving her life, would put Damen's focus back on Scarlet completely. That was something she was reluctant to do, especially in front of Maddy.

"Honestly," Scarlet said unconvincingly, "I think I just want Petula back so that she can make my life hell again."

Charlotte smiled. She could see right through Scarlet's defense mechanisms, directly to her heart.

"This really is so weird, right?" Scarlet said, taking in her surroundings as well as the friendly face in front of her. "Me being here."

It was weird, but totally welcome. Charlotte liked being sucked back into all the gossip at Hawthorne, even under these difficult circumstances. She hadn't felt this good since she'd crossed over. They'd caught up almost completely without ever addressing the most obvious topic of discussion: How, exactly, was Charlotte going to help her?

Maddy, acting like the voice of reason, elbowed into the warm and fuzzy scene again.

"She's just wasting her time here, Charlotte," Maddy warned. "You can't help her."

"You don't know that," Charlotte replied in a surprisingly clipped tone. "Maybe she's here for a reason. Maybe this is *my* reunion."

Maddy just rolled her eyes. Charlotte knew better also but allowed herself a selfish moment under the circumstances.

"If she stays here any longer, it might be," Maddy said, reminding her coldly that time was not on Scarlet's side.

Scarlet was glad to see Charlotte still had the backbone she'd grown the night of the Fall Ball, but Maddy did have a point. Although there was almost nothing she'd rather do than stay and talk with Charlotte, there was still one thing that took precedence, the reason she'd come. Good point or not, however, Scarlet was getting the distinct impression that Maddy was trying to get rid of her and that it had nothing to do with searching for Petula.

"I think she should go," Maddy said emphatically to Charlotte, then glanced over to address Scarlet directly. "Nothing personal, Scarlet, but Petula isn't here *yet*, and you don't belong here either. Yet."

"You said she's in a coma?" Charlotte asked, ignoring Maddy.

"Yeah."

"Well, if she's not quite dead," Charlotte considered, "maybe she's somewhere off-campus, you know, in an intake office, like at . . . the hospital?"

"That's nonsense," Maddy decried. "Dying is not like being on deck in a kickball game."

"Actually," Charlotte said, "it kind of is."

Maddy was totally perplexed, but the look of recognition on Scarlet's face was instant. Dead Ed, the orientation film, the whole Billy and Butch/special abilities kickball metaphor thing. Funny, she thought, that Maddy wouldn't have gotten that too. Everyone had to watch the film. Repeatedly.

"We need to get off campus," Charlotte continued.

"Great. How?" Scarlet asked, eager to just get up and go.

"Charlotte, you can't just head back to the living world," Maddy warned urgently. "You have a job now, responsibilities at the phone bank."

"You mean I might miss one of those calls I never get," Charlotte said sarcastically, but nevertheless understanding that the consequences of venturing off into the unknown could be very dangerous. "I'm sure *you* can handle them for me."

Charlotte's annoyance at Maddy taking her call the other day at work had been festering, and this was as good a time as any for Charlotte to let her know.

"I don't want you to do anything that could hurt you," Scarlet said, feeling guilt and hope in equal measure at the thought

of finally having a solution. "Just point the way, and I'll go on my own."

"No. Our job is to help troubled teens, isn't it?" Charlotte said confidently, looking at Maddy. "You are a troubled teen and I am going to help you."

"Don't you remember all those conversations we had about good deeds?" Maddy scowled, grabbing Charlotte by her scrawny shoulders in a last-ditch effort to talk sense into her. "How pointless they are? What a waste of time they turn out to be?"

"I also told you that I would do *anything* for Scarlet," Charlotte said firmly, staring straight into Maddy's eyes. "Scarlet needs me to go."

"And I need you to stay," Maddy slipped.

The "need" bit was a little jarring for Charlotte to process, and off-putting too. Normally she would have been charmed by Maddy's admitting her vulnerability, her apparent jealousy over Scarlet's visit, like that, but that's not how it came out. It wasn't "need" in the sense of "want" that Maddy was expressing; rather it seemed to be need in the sense of *must*.

"And I need you to mind your own business," Scarlet jabbed.

Charlotte was increasingly pissed that Maddy was sticking her nose in, but she had been a really good friend since they'd arrived, and it was totally understandable that Maddy would feel threatened by her relationship with Scarlet.

"Why don't you come with?" Charlotte suggested. "We could use your help."

"Sorry, Charlotte," Maddy said, "but I'm not going to jeopardize everything by leaving, and you shouldn't either."

Scarlet just frowned knowingly. Maddy didn't appear to her to be someone who would make a sacrifice for any reason.

"No one ever said we can't leave," Charlotte shot back. "Technically, anyway."

Just then, the phone in their apartment rang, and Maddy, using her phone bank skills, jumped to get it.

Maddy turned her back to the girls and nodded a few times, but neither Charlotte nor Scarlet could hear a word she was saying. The girls only knew the chat had ended when Maddy put down the receiver, a much cheerier expression plastered across her face than before.

"Hey, Charlotte, can I borrow you for a minute?" Maddy asked, grabbing her by her waif-like wrist and leading her to another corner of the room.

"You know, at first I thought this might have been a bad idea, with all your work-load and stuff," Maddy chirped, "but I know how unhappy you've been, and going back might, you know, make sense for you," Maddy continued. "I mean, Scarlet's perfect, popular sister is lying there, vulnerable and empty, and you are probably the only one who can help her right now."

"So you're really going to help me?" Charlotte asked.

"That's what friends are for, right?" Maddy affirmed, turning and beaming at Scarlet.

Chapter 13

Shadow of Doubt

Behind every cloud is another cloud.
—Judy Garland

Never trust a person who says *trust me*.

Trust is not a given. In any relationship, it is the hardest thing to earn and the easiest to lose. In fact, the only words harsher than "I don't love you anymore" are "I don't trust you anymore." The former has everything to do with someone else. There is nothing you can do about a change of heart. The latter has everything to do with you.

harlotte, Scarlet, and Maddy arrived at the fenced-in perimeter of the campus as first light fought to break through the overcast sky above them. Up close, the barrier was a bit higher than they expected, but not particularly formidable. There were no guards to avoid or checkpoints to navigate; just a lone video camera like the two at the office.

Charlotte made a kind of climbing motion with her hands, and Scarlet and Maddy caught her drift. Getting up, and even over, was the easy part, Charlotte thought. The backside was a different matter. It was impossible to see much past the fence, even from their apartment. Also, none of them had come in this way, so what really lay on the other side was, at the very least, unknown. At worst, well, nobody wanted to speculate.

"We're off to see Petula . . . ," Charlotte sang nervously.

"I hope you're not betting on a friggin' yellow brick road to lead us there," Maddy said ominously.

Charlotte turned to them, pressed her bony finger to her lips in the universal sign for "shut up," and began climbing stealthily. Scarlet and Maddy followed. The climb down was a lot farther than up, and before long, the dank environs of the campus gave way to the even danker and drearier forest that descended beneath them.

There was no obvious path through mist and the mucky undergrowth, but there was just enough turf wear and light for the girls to see the way.

"Doesn't look like anyone has come this way . . . ," Charlotte noted, and paused at the thought of how best to describe the undefined path. ". . . Lately."

"That's an understatement," Maddy interjected snidely, surveying the little-traveled wood before them.

Scarlet took the lead, stomping over the damp carpet of leaves and dirt. It was invigorating, thrilling even, for Charlotte to be out there with her friends. She imagined that this was what it might be like to go off to college or start an actual life filled with expectations and hope.

At first, the girls all shared a sense of excitement, even Maddy, as they drifted through the forest, blazing a path directly through the Unknown, all three of them together with no one around to tell them what to do or how to do it. It felt like sneaking out in the middle of the night when your parents had gone to bed and having the whole world — and the whole night — to explore.

Scarlet trudged forward, thinking what an amazing game of hide-and-seek she and Petula could've played here as kids. Come to think of it, maybe that is exactly what they were doing now. The stakes were higher though, and the enormity of what they were trying to do began to hit her too.

They trod carefully through the thicket, which sprouted thorns like pimples on an oily face. The little pricks on their legs and arms were getting irritating, and it was getting harder to see. They couldn't really be sure whether they were lost or not.

"This really sucks," Maddy whined to Charlotte so that Scarlet could hear. "Maybe we should turn around."

"Not me," Scarlet retorted, fending off the doubt creeping through her own brain as well. "You can if you want."

"We don't know where we're going," Maddy argued, "or if we can get back."

"I have my own problems." Scarlet grimaced impatiently, reminding Maddy both of her mission and the fact that she wasn't planning on returning anyway. "Besides, you invited yourself."

"I came to help you guys, but if you don't want me here . . ."

"Stop," Charlotte said, nipping the squabble in the bud. "Let's not fight."

Charlotte was playing uniter for Scarlet's sake but was increasingly of a divided mind about this expedition too, and becoming more conflicted with each footstep. There was something about this wasteland surrounding them that was gradually draining her enthusiasm and souring her mood.

It was more than just the physical difficulty of the journey. Her psyche was growing evermore fragile as well, her confidence was shrinking like a cheap sweater in a hot dryer. As unhappy as she'd been lately, this little adventure was proof that things could always get worse. She'd been missing Scarlet and was nostalgic for the good old days of being the resident ghost at Hawthorne High, but maybe it was the idea of Scarlet, of their friendship, that she'd been missing more than the actual person. Perhaps she'd romanticized their relationship to the point where it bore absolutely no resemblance to reality.

She and Maddy were risking a lot to help Scarlet, and Scarlet didn't seem too appreciative. In fact, she had barely looked back to check on them. The other interns' reunions didn't have nearly this kind of downside either. Maybe Charlotte had just gotten sucked in again by all the Damen and Petula talk and made a bad choice.

Maddy reached from behind and put her hand gently on Charlotte's shoulder, as if she'd read her mind.

Scarlet felt herself weakening too, both mind and body, as their progress became slower and slower. She could tell her companions felt the same, and felt them wordlessly blaming her for their plight with each painful stride. The wood had been thickening ever since they left campus, unlike their skins, which were getting thinner by the step. It wasn't that any of these girls was particularly sensitive, it's that their nerves had become almost unbearably frayed, rubbed raw by both the harsh landscape and each other. In fact, the girls had barley spoken a word among them since their stressful tiff

earlier, and Scarlet was starting to feel like the odd soul out in this spectral threesome.

That Scarlet didn't like Maddy, and vice versa, was a massive understatement, Scarlet thought, and it was clearly making Charlotte uncomfortable. In her own defense, Scarlet reasoned, it wasn't really that she didn't like her, it was just that Maddy's even being with them felt intrusive.

This was the only time she might ever have with Charlotte again, and she didn't want to share it with some pushy stranger. As far as Scarlet was concerned, Maddy had totally earjacked their most private conversations and hacked into their friendship. How, Scarlet thought, after all they'd been through, could Charlotte let that happen?

Just as things were at their grimmest, between the travelers, and the foliage, and their nerve endings, Scarlet spied a clearing.

A few steps farther and they emerged from the thicket, right at the fork of two clearly marked roads, one overgrown and little-trod, the other manicured and worn.

"Here we are," Scarlet observed sarcastically, "at the proverbial fork in the road." She walked up to the fork and closed her eyes, trying desperately to channel her gut. She was waiting for her intuition to kick in, but it must have been on a coffee break, because all she felt was paralyzed.

"I have no idea," Scarlet admitted, in a rare show of insecurity. "You guys make the decision."

"We need to go left," Maddy chirped decisively, signaling the direction.

"I agree," Charlotte said just as self-assuredly. She really

had no idea and simply mustered whatever faith remained in her own judgment to support Maddy's choice.

"How do you know?" Scarlet asked Charlotte, questioning not just Maddy's suggestion but Charlotte's deference as well.

This kind of confrontation was new territory for them both. Trust had always been the strongest bond between them.

"I just do," Charlotte trumpeted suspiciously. "I feel it."

Scarlet tried to keep her cool, but with Petula's life, and her own, at stake, it was getting harder by the second. Doubt was flooding her mind like water in a sinking ship. She had nothing to base a decision on but her faith in Charlotte, and that was being sorely tested right now. She walked over to Charlotte and took it up a notch.

"When was the last time you were right about your instinct?" Scarlet asked.

"I was right about you," Charlotte said calmly. "I knew you were special, and I knew you belonged with Damen." It still hurt her just a little to speak those words. But Scarlet heard something entirely different in her head. Scarlet heard, "You owe me."

"Yeah, well, looks like you just might have been wrong on both accounts," Scarlet said.

Charlotte was stung but tried hard to let it slide. The two of them bickering was unnatural, sort of like a comedian heckling himself. She got that Scarlet needed, and deserved, a more independent opinion from her right now, but she was at a loss. Maddy seemed much more certain than she was, Charlotte thought, and the path to the left definitely seemed the easier and more popular route.

"I guess there's no way to know until we actually make the choice," Charlotte said, acquiescing. "I think we should go left."

"*You* think?" Scarlet said dryly.

Scarlet saw the hurt look on Charlotte's face and wondered if she was just being unreasonable. None of them knew which road to take. How could they? Wasn't her resistance simply due to the fact that Maddy had suggested it? Regardless, she thought, Charlotte's uncertainty was not very much help to her at this critical time, and she was more than a little disappointed that her friend seemed so easily bullied by her and influenced by Maddy.

"What are we waiting for?" Maddy asked, challenging Scarlet for a decision.

"Follow me," Maddy instructed, grabbing Charlotte's arm and heading left.

Scarlet went right. Alone.

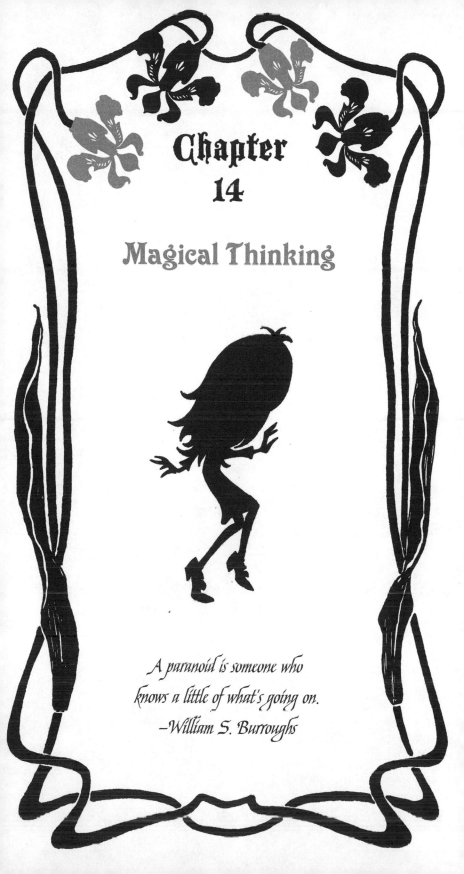

Chapter 14

Magical Thinking

A paranoid is someone who
knows a little of what's going on.
—William S. Burroughs

What doesn't kill you makes you paranoid.

Trapped in your own head, without an exit strategy, conflicted by doubt and with only your obsessions to guide you, reality takes a backseat to anxiety, changing shape faster than a Coney Island contortionist. Charlotte and Scarlet both were realizing that the worst place to be lost was in your own head.

**P**hones were ringing off the hook at the call center and everyone was pretty distracted by the fact that Charlotte hadn't shown up. They tried to keep it down so that Mr. Markov wouldn't hear.

"Did she really try to call in sick?" Pam asked, astonished.

"Yep," Prue signaled, covering the receiver on her conversation.

"Is Maddy with her?" Suzy Scratcher mouthed to Kim.

"She's not here," Kim said hurriedly, working two phone lines at once.

As the expression on Prue's face changed from disbelief to worry all the chatter in the room quieted. She hung up the phone and looked over at Pam.

"We have to go."

⁂

Charlotte watched helplessly as Scarlet's bouncing black bob disappeared down the right-hand path and back into the forest.

"Scarlet," Charlotte called several times without a response.

Maddy held Charlotte's arm tightly, stopping her from chasing after Scarlet.

"I wanted to go right," Charlotte mumbled apologetically. "But I hesitated. I just couldn't be sure."

"Don't stress. She'll be all right."

"You don't know that," Charlotte agonized. "She's out there by herself. Probably scared half to death."

"She's more than half dead already."

"That's not funny," Charlotte said. "I think we should go after her before she gets in too deep."

"If we really want to help Scarlet, we should get to that hospital."

Charlotte knew that leaving Scarlet on her own was not something a best friend would do, but not leaving might mean an even worse fate for Petula. Scarlet was tough, Charlotte thought, and street smart. She'd find her way if anyone could.

Charlotte nodded at Maddy, looked down the right side of the path, made a wish for Scarlet to travel safely, and walked to the left to find Petula.

ॐ

"Someone is coming!" Virginia shrieked as if they were game show castaways waiting to be whisked off the island to a five-star hotel where they could bathe and eat to their hearts' content.

"No, there isn't," Petula said, peering through the glass windows of the office and down the hallway.

She didn't see anyone. Not a discharge nurse, doctor, or orderly. No one. Still, having no reason to doubt Virginia, she put her ear to the ground and began to hear the faint echo of footsteps as well.

"I didn't say I heard buffalo."

"Shhh . . . ," Petula said, hushing Virginia and backing her into a little closet nook. "I have a weird feeling."

Blazing a rough path through the trees and bushes that surrounded her, Scarlet felt as if she were in a modern art museum with impressionist portraits all around her. She could tell the subject from a distance, but up close, it all just looked like spilled, splattered paint.

She couldn't be sure if it was fear in her mind or if her eyes were playing tricks on her, but it didn't really matter. She was all alone and totally unsure of anything: where she was, where she was going, and how she was going to get there.

This wasn't the old Scarlet, and she knew it. She hadn't been since she'd become so insecure about Damen, and those doubts had infected her thoughts, her decisions, and her other relationships.

"Make decisions for yourself, not because of a guy," her mother had warned her over and over again.

Petula would never listen, not that it mattered. When she looked into a guy's eyes, she was only looking for her own reflection anyway. But Scarlet had listened. At least until recently. There was no point in kidding herself any longer though. Saving Petula was important, but that was really the doctors' job. Saving her relationship was what she was after, and she was ashamed by the realization. Had all this drama just been her way of getting his attention after all or . . . keeping it?

She thought about how she stormed away from her one true friend, and how she was not only lost now but had been

lost for quite some time. She was alienating the people that she loved, consumed with the insecurities that came a la carte with her relationship with Damen.

She could only trust his word that he wanted to be with one person and one person alone — her. He never gave her reason to believe otherwise, but considering he left Petula for her, she could never really be sure. He would argue that he never loved Petula, but to Scarlet, that might have even been worse.

❧

"How are they doing, doctor?" Damen asked hopefully.

"No change," Dr. Patrick responded.

It was getting a little old, but Damen took this neutral evaluation as confirmation that both girls were still stable. Cranial X-rays, PET scans, and MRI films were hanging on light boxes like subway ads, all negative as far as he'd been told. There hadn't been any major episodes all day. No need to intubate, inject, or resuscitate either of them.

They both looked peaceful, as if they might be resting comfortably, except for the drain attached to Petula's infected toe and the ankle cuffs preventing blood clots in both their legs, which didn't look like fun. The metronomic inflation and deflation of the cuffs had become a source of comfort to Damen, who played a little game with himself, synching their breathing, and marking time to their airflow in and out.

Damen walked over to Scarlet's bedside and knocked accidentally into the moveable table on which rested a small bouquet of flowers he'd purchased at the hospital gift shop and a pitcher of unused water. He noticed that the spilled water was

pooling and was just about to hit a penlight that Dr. Patrick must have left behind during her examination. Damen rescued the gadget, sat down next to Scarlet, and began fidgeting with the light, clicking it on and off, trying desperately to think of a way to bring her back.

It was getting to be too much for even him. All this speculating, observing, worrying, and waiting. It was all so passive. His head was getting tired and he needed to clear it. Damen walked over to the nearby nurses' station and asked about the little girl he'd seen earlier.

"What happened?" he asked quietly, so as not to disturb her family.

"Car accident," the nurse said, looking up from her paperwork. "On the way back from some contest or something . . . the poor little thing."

A million thoughts raced through Damen's mind. He imagined how happy the girl must have been, all dressed up, and how proud her parents must have been. And then in a second, without warning, it was all taken away. He couldn't stop himself from thinking something trivial at the same time. He hoped she'd won.

"How is she doing?" Damen asked, fearing he already knew the answer.

"Nothing more we can do now," the nurse advised kindly, "except pray."

Damen let that last bit sink in, especially in terms of his own situation. He stopped outside the little girl's room, said a silent prayer for her, and walked back to the Kensington girls' room, intent on leaving his passive self behind.

Chapter 15

Pretty Vacant

A narcissist is someone better looking than you.
—Gore Vidal

A little vanity
goes a long way.

———◆━◆◆◆━◆———

Some people think everything they do is
great and that they always look fabulous,
even if they don't. They have this ability
to be a cheerleader for themselves, even if
they're on a losing team. Narcissists trade
reality for fantasy. Rather than displaying a
dysfunctional personality disorder, however,
they are the ones who have it all figured out.
The only world that matters is the one you
create, the one you choose to live in. Petula
had worked that out a long time ago.

 have a question . . . ," Virginia said as she watched Petula twisting her long, faux-blond hair into a perfectly messy knot.

"They're real."

"Why are we in hospital gowns?" Virginia asked, completely ignoring Petula's arrogance.

"I don't really know. But less really is more, isn't it?"

"I'm being serious."

"Okay, seriously, then," Petula enunciated sarcastically. "We are wearing hospital gowns because we are in a hospital!"

"Duh!" Virginia mocked. "My point is, *why*. I don't remember being sick."

Come to think of it, neither did Petula. In fact, the only thing she remembered was collapsing on her driveway, but that was not something she planned to discuss with the kid. She assumed that Scarlet had probably dragged her, disgustedly,

to bed, but she couldn't be sure of that either, and she didn't remember being taken to the hospital to get her stomach pumped or anything.

"It doesn't matter how I got here," Petula said, avoiding the question entirely. "I have health insurance."

"But why are we alone here?"

"We're not alone," Petula said emphatically. "The nurse will be here to discharge us any minute."

"How do you know? We've been waiting a long time."

Virginia's questions were making Petula increasingly uneasy. Not just because she didn't have answers but because they were questions she'd been asking herself since she arrived.

"We heard footsteps, didn't we?"

"Yeah," Virginia acknowledged, the façade of fierceness she'd been wearing giving way to a trembling lip. "But what if they weren't the nurses' footsteps?"

Petula hadn't fully entertained that possibility until now, and the suddenly fearful expression on her face gave her away to Virginia.

Petula wasn't very touchy-feely or very good in the eye-contact department. One could even argue, and some therapists had, that she was afflicted with Asperger's Syndrome, a mild form of autism that made any kind of social interaction for her . . . challenging.

But the truth was her issues weren't anything near as interesting or deep as that. She was just self-absorbed. This was proven when, as a five-year-old, mistakenly diagnosed with A.D.D., she spent three hours at the mall debating between

coral or burnt orange shoes to wear for the first day of kindergarten.

"Don't worry," Petula reassured Virginia in the only way she knew how, "I'll be at Homecoming if it kills me."

∂∽

"Scarlet," Damen pleaded, flashing the narrow beam of light from the laser pen Dr. Patrick had left behind in her eyes. "Please come back."

He held her lids open gently and studied her pupils closely for any reaction. All he could think about was how happy she always was to see him. How he could always get her eyes to light up just by saying her name, but now they were just dark holes.

He tossed the penlight on the floor with frustration and grabbed the desk lamp clipped to Scarlet's headboard. He brought it right up to her face and shined it in her eyes until the inside of her nostrils glowed orange from the wattage.

"Please, Scarlet," he begged, his voice cracking. "Come back.

"Come back to me."

∂∽

Trapped in the middle of nowhere, literally, without a friend in sight and feeling closer to death by the minute, Scarlet was trying hard to channel her old self. Not that she was ever particularly cheery or upbeat, but she'd always prided herself

on her determination, defiance, and independent streak. All those qualities were in short supply right about now with little hope of restocking before the final closeout sale. Nevertheless, she still had enough pride left to beat back the tears she felt swelling in her eyes, attempt to regroup, and do whatever she could to find her way back to the hospital.

She tossed her hair away from her face, raised her head from its hiding place between her arms, and, looking off in the distance through the tangle of leafless branches, she saw a light. She couldn't quite tell what it was, but she knew it was not the moon or a twinkling star — it was too steady for that. Whatever it was, she felt compelled to walk toward it, and after a few yards the stream of light became a blinding flash. It lit everything around her, most importantly a detour she must have overlooked the first time.

She walked down the new pathway and felt just as lost as before until she began to hear the sound of twigs and branches cracking.

"Charlotte?" she called out reticently, hoping her friend had indeed come to her rescue.

"Charlotte?" the voice called back faintly.

Scarlet froze. It wasn't Charlotte, but it wasn't an echo either. It wasn't her voice at all, in fact. The whole black forest thing was weird enough, but now it was getting downright terrifying. Scarlet heard loud footsteps running toward her, and she panicked. That shining light must have been a trick, and she'd fallen for it, like a rookie.

She did her best not to fall down, screaming helplessly like one of those high-heeled victims in slasher films — she did

not want to go out like that — but it didn't matter. She felt something take hold of one of her ankles and pull her to the ground like a rodeo calf. There was something oddly familiar about the grip.

"Oh, no," the voice above her moaned. "Not again" was all Scarlet could hear as her face hit dirt and her body flipped over onto her back, eyes closed tightly, waiting for the ax to fall.

Scarlet was frozen; her limbs went dead as if she were just zapped by a Taser.

"Prue?" Scarlet asked, peeking through squinted eyelids.

Prue released her from the leg tackle she'd just employed and stood over her in disbelief.

"Pam?" Scarlet asked a little more hopefully, looking to Prue's side.

Both girls nodded, the look of disbelief on their faces noticeable.

"What are *you* doing here?" the girls asked each other, laughing and then hugging before any bothered to answer.

❧

The rest of Charlotte and Maddy's walk had been easy, like a stroll around the manicured grounds of some well-kept historic estate, but Charlotte's mind was restless.

"Maddy, do you think she'll be okay?"

"Hard to say," Maddy said ambivalently. "It's too bad you guys had to fight after not seeing each other for so long."

"I know. She came all this way to find me, and now she's lost."

"She was always kind of difficult though, right?" Maddy asked rhetorically. "Kind of selfish?"

"I guess."

"She grew up the same as Petula," Maddy said. "Nice house, nice family, every advantage."

"Yes, what's your point?"

"My point is that all the drama and sourpussing around is an act," Maddy answered. "To get what she wants."

Maddy had really gotten to an issue that Charlotte had wondered about since she first met Scarlet. She'd always assumed that Scarlet's personality and attitude were just a reaction to Petula's. But maybe it was really just Scarlet's way of getting attention.

"I mean, think about it," Maddy went on. "She stole her sister's boyfriend and used you to get him."

"She didn't steal him," Charlotte said weakly. "Not exactly."

"Is that right?"

"I helped her get him, even though I . . ."

"Wanted him?" Maddy concluded. "Now she comes here to use you again, only this time for you to save her sister, who treated you like dirt."

"Scarlet's not like that. She's impulsive. She gets carried away sometimes, that's all."

"Stop making excuses for her," Maddy interjected. "You deserve better than the way she's treated you."

Charlotte really didn't appreciate the way Maddy was talking about Scarlet, but then, she couldn't really rebut anything she was saying. Scarlet *did* have it really easy. Much easier than Charlotte had. Scarlet might not have been popular like

Petula, but that was her choice. She could have been. She preferred to rebel, be different, and it still got her noticed, didn't it?

They strolled a short while longer and then spied a town in the distance.

"That's Hawthorne," Charlotte said with awe, as if she'd just spotted The Emerald City.

It was home. Her home. Maybe not sweet, but bittersweet at least. The place where she dreamed her dreams, made her plans but never got to live them. The place that she had left behind, the people too. People she would never, ever forget, but how long before they'd forget her, she continued to wonder.

"I told you this was the best way."

"You were right," Charlotte acknowledged, "about everything."

Chapter 16

Bizarre Love Triangle

This wasn't supposed to happen.
I've been hit with your charm.
How could you do this to me?
I'm in love again.
—The Sugarcubes

Don't tempt me.

———◆◆◆◆◆———

We all want what we can't have. In fact, most of the time we only want things because they are unavailable or forbidden. To justify the purchase, we convince ourselves that what we want so desperately is also what we need. The trouble is, impulse purchases can often lead to an expensive case of buyer's remorse.

carlet was waving her hands wildly in the dank air as she explained everything to Prue and Pam. She told them about Petula and her botched pedicure, how desperate the situation was, and why she had come. Once they were all on the same page and had gotten over the initial shock of seeing each other again, the conversation quickly turned to Charlotte.

"When she called in sick . . . ," Pam said, "we got really suspicious."

"So we went to her apartment to drag her in to work," Prue explained.

Scarlet sensed there was more they weren't telling her, but she let it go for now.

"What's weird is we were looking for Charlotte," Prue said, "and we found you."

The girls stood looking at each other for a second, chewing

over the circumstances that had thrown them together once again.

"We've been feeling pretty bad about not having a lot of time for her," Prue lamented. "But things are different now than they were in Dead Ed."

"That's only part of the problem, anyway," Pam let slip.

"What's the other part?" Scarlet asked. "Or maybe I should say *who*."

Pam and Prue knew exactly what Scarlet meant. Everyone was suspicious of Maddy, even Scarlet, who barely knew her.

"She's a nightmare," Scarlet railed.

"Tell us about it," Prue concurred. "Maybe worse."

"She's been feeding all of Charlotte's insecurities about not being reunited," Pam said. "And keeping her away from her old friends."

"I'm sure when you showed up," Prue said, "Maddy freaked out."

"Yeah, she got a little passive-aggressive, but then she offered to help us find Petula."

"Really?" Pam asked, shooting Prue a knowing look. "Where were you headed?"

"To the hospital."

"Let's go," Prue ordered. "Now."

❦

"There it is," Charlotte said, pointing excitedly to the tall building in the distance.

"C'mon," Maddy smiled giddily, grabbing Charlotte's hand and hurrying her along.

They meandered through the small town, Charlotte turning her head from side to side, accessing memories, some good, most bad, at nearly every street corner and shop. Down Main Street, they passed by the nail salon and saw the makeshift pre-morial for Petula.

"Wow," Maddy said, getting Charlotte's attention, "she must be really popular!"

"You have no idea," Charlotte replied quietly, taking in the burning candles, notes, and mound of colorful get well bouquets spilling from the salon doorway onto the sidewalk. Charlotte was good at erecting mental memorials, but seeing an actual, real-life one for Petula was a little too much to take.

"You must have been cool too, right?" Maddy's comment hit Charlotte like the sight of a magazine page that has you and another girl wearing the same outfit and 88 percent of the readers voted that she wore it better.

Charlotte remembered her own memorial. It wasn't even the bargain bin version of Petula's.

"Yeah. They had buses for the service and everything."

She conveniently left out the fact that the buses didn't exactly make it to the service, but whatever. She was the reason for a half day, and that practically meant her death was recognized as a holiday. This made her feel a little bit better anyway, but the lack of enthusiasm was noticeable to Maddy, who didn't feel the need to press it any further.

They walked, unseen, into the busy Emergency entrance of the hospital and behind the nurses' station desk, looking for Petula's room.

"Third floor," Maddy said, fingering the patient roster. "Room three-three-three."

❧

Damen was slumped in his chair, situated between Petula and Scarlet, half asleep, when the floor nurse brushed by and woke him. She was there to sponge-bathe the girls, Scarlet first, so Damen moved to a chair closer to the door. The nurse pulled the curtain between the beds closed to give Scarlet some privacy, which Damen appreciated. All the poking and prodding of his girlfriend by strangers, even though they were medical professionals, was really starting to get to him. It was all so undignified.

The drawn curtain gave him very little to look at except Petula, which was something he had not done much of since his vigil began. Staring over her immobile form, he couldn't help but notice how good she still looked. So much of Petula was about the surface that it wasn't really shocking to him that her looks would be the last thing to break down.

She'd been at death's door since he arrived, but for the first time, he could actually envision her being dead. He pictured her in a coffin, the frilly lining studiously color-coordinated with her outfit, her spiked high heels thrusting defiantly upward at the bottom, and her class ring gleaming from her folded fingers, as a line of mourners waited eagerly to view her corpse. He was glad not to be able to see Scarlet right now with his mind wandering like this. Even in a coma, she might know what he was thinking.

He looked away from Petula and around her bed, where only a single bouquet of flowers from her mother sat. Now that was odd. He'd heard about the memorial sprouting up around the nail salon, and all the chatter around town, but nobody had come to see Petula except the Wendys, and that barely counted, their motivation being so suspect. Public grieving, like the memorial, was not really a good barometer of affection because it was always more about the spectacle than the deceased anyway.

That was always the problem with being Petula, Damen thought. She was popular, but not liked, if such a thing was possible. Other people wanted Petula to like *them*, notice *them*, not the other way around. Now that she couldn't provide that positive reenforcement to others by inviting them to her parties, hanging out with them, or actually remembering their names, she was kind of like a passé child star grown out of her cutesy roles. All she could do for them now was die, the quicker the better, to make her fans feel better about themselves for caring and provide a last little bit of entertainment for everyone while she was still hot. Talk about undignified, he thought.

Damen walked over to Petula, not out of remorse per se, but out of guilt. He'd made the right decision being with Scarlet, that was for sure, but he'd probably handled it the wrong way. No matter how arrogant Petula acted at the time, she was a human being and she had been humiliated. Some might even say she suffered, not that her pride would ever let it show.

He took Petula's French-manicured hand uncomfortably in his for the first time in ages and leaned over her, saying the words he probably should have said a long time ago.

"I'm sorry," Damen whispered.

Just then, Maddy and Charlotte entered in the room. The sight of Damen cooing in Petula's ear was a shocker.

"Look at that," Maddy said, as if cheering on a TV soap romance. "He still loves her."

Charlotte was speechless as all the old feelings came flooding back and seeing him again made her heart melt like a Dreamsicle stuck to a dashboard on a hot summer day. He was still golden and gorgeous, and now so gentle and vulnerable. It was as if he literally hotwired her heart. Not even death could hold back those familiar feelings. They didn't have anything to do with her body or her head; they were imprinted in her soul.

"That's Damen," Charlotte said to Maddy like a lovesick schoolgirl.

The truth was, Charlotte was wiser, more mature, but she would never get older, and her deep, heart-on-her-sleeve emotions would always be with her. Seeing Damen took her back to a place where she had her whole life in front of her. Where anything was possible. B.G. — Before Gummy. She longed for that time again, a time of innocence and hope, a time before she was trapped in eternal teendom.

Maddy's gaze shifted from Charlotte to Damen and back, taking the measure of each. Charlotte's distress was plain to see.

"Don't be so surprised," Maddy mumbled under her breath, but loud enough for Charlotte to hear. "Guys are only as faithful as their options."

"He's not like that!"

"I wonder what Scarlet would think?" Maddy asked rhetorically. "It's a good thing we got here first."

"Yeah," Charlotte said absentmindedly. "Good thing . . ."

Maddy was talking about Scarlet, but Charlotte couldn't stop thinking about herself. She was fixated on the romantic scene before her, unable to resist inserting herself again, much as she had once before.

"Was it really worth giving him up for Scarlet?" Maddy prodded. "Just so that he could go back to Petula?"

"I don't know. I thought so at the time."

"No good deed goes unpunished. That's what I always say."

Charlotte knew a lot about unintended consequences. She'd been a victim of them since choking on that damn piece of candy. All she ever really wanted was to be popular, like Petula, and be noticed by Damen. Not dead, like she wound up. Not waiting for some supernatural phone to ring or some whining, coddled teenager to call in with a pathetic little problem.

Damen stood up and looked warmly at Petula. Charlotte did too. She looked good. Tanned, toned, same as always. Helpless, though, that was a new one.

"She isn't much use to him like this," Maddy commented. "Is she?"

"What do you mean?"

"Don't you see?" Maddy paused for effect and gestured at Petula like a game show prize. "You could have everything you ever wanted."

As Damen moved away from Petula, Charlotte moved within arms' distance of her. She studied her, watched her chest rise and fall faintly with each labored breath. Maybe it would be the decent thing to do, Charlotte thought, bringing Petula back to life. She was sure to die if they couldn't find her soul, but there was no guarantee that was going to happen.

"Who would ever know?" Maddy pushed, feeling Charlotte teeter. "It would be the greatest comeback ever."

"I could never do that to Scarlet," Charlotte said, trying to shake some sort of sense back into her own head.

Charlotte looked and felt like she was stuck in a corner of a boxing ring, being pelted.

"Look, we don't even know if Scarlet is going to come back at all," Maddy said. "Think of her mother — at least one of her daughters could be spared. You'd be doing a good thing, a selfless thing."

Charlotte felt somber at the idea that Scarlet may never come back, but she was beginning to catch Maddy's drift, and it scared her. She'd tried to possess Petula once before, and as she recalled, it didn't go very well. Still, the possibility of a do-over remained intriguing.

Come to think of it, things had only really gone wrong for her when she'd failed to possess Petula and had to possess Scarlet instead. If not for that, Scarlet and Damen might never have gotten to know each other, let alone hook up. It wasn't so

much that they were meant to be, Charlotte rationalized, as the fact that she'd thrown them together, like two characters in a war-time romance brought together by fate, but destined ultimately to be apart.

"What about Scarlet," Charlotte asked halfheartedly, running her hands just inches over Petula's body.

"What about her? If for some reason she does come back, which I'm not sure she will, she'll get what she wants . . . mostly."

"Petula," Charlotte replied, "but maybe not Damen."

"She'll have to face the truth sooner or later anyway," Maddy touted. "It's obvious he doesn't really love her."

It was hard for Charlotte to argue with Maddy's logic. Perhaps all that angst Scarlet told her she was feeling was not imaginary. Maybe they'd just grown apart and Damen was feeling a little buyer's remorse but was too decent to admit it. At least if she possessed Petula, reanimated her, she might be doing not just Scarlet or Damen but the whole world a favor. Just imagine, she thought, if Petula could use all those genetic gifts for good instead of for planning to be someone's future ex-wife with a huge divorce settlement and one of those pretentious little dogs for a "child." Maybe possessing her now would be a mission of mercy for all mankind. She looked over at Damen sitting there staring at Petula and felt empowered.

Charlotte reached for Petula's chest and placed her hand over her heart, in preparation to recite the incantation, when suddenly the floor nurse pulled away the curtain that had been

hiding Scarlet's body. The sound broke Charlotte's concentration, and when she looked over, the sight of Scarlet, lying there so pale and vulnerable, brought her back to her senses.

"I can't do this," she said to Maddy, wiping at her eyes as if she'd just woken from a deep sleep.

❧

Scarlet, Pam, and Prue were finally making some progress. The tangle of branches, dead leaves, and heavy mist gave way to a forest of short stumps and light fog.

"Charlotte and Maddy were headed for the hospital, right?" Pam asked Scarlet.

"I think so. That was the only info I had to give them."

"Maybe that's a good thing," Prue responded.

"What do you mean?"

"They'll probably go to her hospital room, where her body is," Pam conjectured, "But her spirit won't be there."

Scarlet thought about it for a second and realized her own body was there, too. It creeped her out to think that Maddy might be staring at her, judging her.

"Where will it be, then?" Scarlet asked, totally confused.

"In the hospital intake office," Prue said. "Wherever that is."

"Everyone has to pass through an intake office," Pam explained, "on their way over."

"I didn't. I went straight to Dead Ed."

"That's because you aren't deceased, Scarlet," Prue quipped, the disapproval in her voice showing.

"How do we find the office?" Scarlet said.

"Good question," Pam answered. "Only kids who have passed through it know where it is and can get back there."

"But chances are good that one of the kids in that class came through the hospital," Prue continued, picking up Pam's thread. "Do you know where it is?"

"I do," Scarlet puffed.

Chapter 17

Tomorrow Never Knows

*Life is about not knowing, having to change,
taking the moment and making the best of it,
without knowing what's going to happen next.*
—Gilda Radner

We only fear
what we don't know.

—◆◆◆—

Yet fear is what makes us feel most alive. Familiarity breeds comfort, the Unknown breeds doubt. Will this be your last sunset? Will you ever eat ice cream again? Will you ever feel again the way he makes you feel right now? The uncertainty keeps us on the rim, sharp, living in suspense, at the edge of possibility. Charlotte knew that she had something inside of her that she wanted back, but what exactly that was, she did not know.

endy Anderson and Wendy Thomas showed up at the nurses' station, dressed to kill in fitted couture suits.

"Do you know how long it will be?" Wendy Thomas asked the charge nurse, as if they were waiting for a table to open up at an exclusive club.

"There's no wait," the nurse replied helpfully. "You can go right in."

"No," Wendy Anderson clarified, "we mean, how much *longer* will it be?"

"There is no change in their status," she said tersely after reviewing their charts and the girls' outfits. "Names, please."

The Wendys handed over their IDs, but the nurse, like everyone else who ever proofed them, was barely able to tell their pictures apart.

She looked the girls over and quickly wrote the first initials

of their last names on their visitors' tags: "T" & "A."
She handed them over to the girls with a slight smirk on
her face.

"Who says nurses aren't smart enough to be doctors?"
Wendy Anderson jabbed.

The two glamazons wiped the artificial concern off their
professionally made-up faces and galumphed uncertainly on
their new heels to the Kensington girls' room. Their focus was
shifting away from Petula's condition to more selfish matters,
namely the official line of Homecoming succession. They'd
been functioning as vice presidents in Petula's cabinet for
a long time, and given the unfortunate circumstances, one
of them would be the logical choice to fulfill her Homecoming duties.

They felt entitled after their successful lobbying effort at
the local Chevy dealer for a brand-new Corvette for the
Homecoming queen to take her victory lap around the track.
All they had to do was trade a little skin, appearing at the local
car show in bikinis for some cheesecake pictures with random
geeks and pervs — something they would have done for nothing if they'd been asked anyway. Either Petula was going
to make it or not, and by "make it," the Wendys meant, "to
Homecoming," not necessarily back to consciousness.

Charlotte looked away from Scarlet's bed as the Wendys
traipsed into the room. She was mesmerized by them as
she had been in life. Maddy, too, was momentarily distracted by the duo. She sized them up instantly to gauge their
level of sophistication and concluded that she did not feel
threatened.

The Wendys definitely did not have anything like resurrection, or resuscitation, for that matter, on their agenda as their clacking heels announced their arrival and roused Damen from his stupor.

Damen lifted his head and rubbed his eyes to focus, and was instantly disgusted by the Wendys' appearance. It was obvious to him that one or both of them were more than ready to accept the honor of Homecoming queen on Petula's behalf.

"You couldn't even wait until the body was cold, could you?" Damen said in disdain.

"You're the one playing musical sisters," Wendy Anderson snapped. "This is what Petula would have wanted."

"Yeah, we're doing it for her," Wendy Thomas echoed, reaching for the hanger holding Petula's dress and stretching it across her body for effect. "It would just kill her if someone else got the crown."

"How considerate of them," Maddy whispered to Charlotte.

"Yes," Charlotte acknowledged, missing her sarcasm entirely once again.

Leave it to those two to find the silver lining in someone else's misfortune, Damen thought. He stared intensely over at the Wendys for an uncomfortably long while. And then it occurred to him. The most outlandish, ridiculous thing he'd ever thought, but just possibly the answer to his prayers.

"You know what, you're right," Damen said with a crazed look in his eyes. "The crown shouldn't go to anyone else."

Everyone was confused, even Charlotte. Maddy stiffened up to listen more intently.

"If anything will bring her back, it's Homecoming," Damen said, reasoning it out more for his own benefit than the Wendys'. "And if she comes back, Scarlet comes back."

"Is there a loony bin in this place?" Wendy Anderson asked indelicately. "I hear psych wards are the new rehab."

Charlotte suddenly found herself wondering if a visit to the funny farm might not be such a bad idea for her either, considering the way she'd been thinking about possessing Petula and having Damen all to herself. The truth was, she wasn't really thinking and really hadn't been since crossing over. She was just allowing herself to be carried along and carried away, by Maddy mostly, who continued to make the case for full body takeover relentlessly.

"Charlotte, this is your time!" Maddy yelled in her face, trying to shake her into action. "If he takes her out of here, she'll die."

Charlotte, rather, seemed to be sloughing off Maddy's argument instead. At least for the moment. She stopped listening to Maddy and started watching Damen closely. She was beginning to get it.

Damen grabbed the portable monitor that they used to take Petula for tests and started to put it around her wrist.

No, I can't put it here, someone will see it, he thought to himself.

"What are you doing?" Wendy Thomas asked.

"I got it! I'll just put it around her ankle and it will look like an alcohol monitor," Damen said. "I'm sure she won't be the only girl in the Homecoming court to have one of those."

Both Wendys stared at each other, devising an exit strategy, telepathically, to stop this madness. Sharing a brain came in handy in situations like these. Suddenly, they both bolted for the door. Damen, too, as he tried to stop them. The door slammed shut before any of them could get to it, thanks to Charlotte. Damen slammed his foot against it and turned to face the Wendys, not entirely sure what had just happened, but very glad it did.

"Nice work," Maddy said, hoping Charlotte had been persuaded to keep them all in place for a big Petula revival.

Charlotte, caught up in the scene playing out in front of them, didn't acknowledge her.

"Nobody leaves this room until I say so," Damen barked commandingly while shooting his eyes around the room searching for the invisible doorman.

"How are you going to get her out of here? You can't just drag her lifeless body out and slap her in a Corvette," Wendy Thomas said, realizing that what she just said was pretty much an oxymoron.

"You'll get arrested," Wendy Anderson said, much more to the point.

Damen wasn't listening anymore, if he ever had been in the first place. He propped Petula up, grabbed some "Facial Freeze" cream out of Wendy's bag, applied a generous amount to Petula's orbital area, and held open her eyes for a second while the cream set.

"Hey, wait, that stuff is expensive! It's liquid gold. Botox in a bottle!"

Damen then applied some around her mouth and fixed a smile on her face, finishing off the look by waving her arm manually back and forth.

"Okay, well, it looks good now, but . . . ," Wendy Thomas said, defeated.

Finally Damen reached for the back of Petula's neck to untie her smock. The Wendys eyes widened, but they were too afraid to try to restrain him.

"Look at that, they're back together and going to the big Homecoming dance," Maddy whispered in Charlotte's ear. "And he's almost got her clothes off already!"

Charlotte looked over at Scarlet's body lying serenely in the midst of all this chaos and seeming infidelity, hurting for her.

Then, Damen stepped away, incredibly uncomfortable at the thought of holding Petula's naked body in his arms. He quickly ripped her sparkling pink frock, which looked more like a dress that should have been worn by some celebriteen du jour to a couture fashion show rather than to a high school homecoming ceremony, from the Wendys' clutches and unsuccessfully tried to dress her.

"Help me," Damen asked softly, expressing vulnerability to the Wendys for the first and probably only time in his life.

Both girls refused, not just to spite him but to preserve whatever might be left of their Homecoming hopes; besides, they didn't want to be upstaged by Petula's beautiful gown when they were wearing suits.

"Fine," Damen said, struggling to hold up Petula's dead weight while shooting them a "remind me later why I'm going

to kill you" look. He then glanced over at Scarlet for permission or forgiveness, probably both, and said, "I'll do it."

Damen strategically used her hospital gown to keep her covered up as best he could and carefully rolled the train of the gown up in his hands, trying and failing to slip the tight, hand-beaded bodice over her head. He needed to keep her arms raised and with her body limp, it was hard to do without assistance. And then he got some.

As Damen held Petula's arms up for a second try, Charlotte moved close to him, nudging his hand and the dress into position, as she had once guided his hand for the Physics exam. With Charlotte's help, the silken dress slid down around Petula perfectly. She stepped back again as Maddy snuggled up to her once more.

"That dress would look even more beautiful on you," Maddy said. "You're the one who deserves to go, and I bet he'd much rather be with you."

Charlotte couldn't help but agree but the Wendys' shrill voices shocked her back in the moment as they made one last ditch effort to reason with Damen.

"You have to get her past the nurses' station and security, not to mention everyone in the hall," Wendy Thomas said, desperately, trying to protect her shot at the crown. "There's no way."

"Want to bet?" Charlotte said.

Chapter 18

Alone Again Or

*Solitude sails in a wave of
forgiveness on angels' wings.*
—Siouxsie Sioux

It's not you, it's me.

———◆·◇·◆———

These are the most dreaded words spoken in any relationship. If you hear them, or if you find yourself wanting to say them, you can be pretty sure it's over. A soft landing is being prepared, but the end result is not in question. Whoever offers this duplicitous explanation on the way out may not be sure of what they want exactly, but they are sure of what they don't want—you.

'm afraid," Virginia blurted out as Petula finished putting little ringlets in her long, flowing hair by spitting a little on her finger, twisting the strands tightly like she would a phone cord, and then releasing the bouncy curls.

"I am too."

These were the words both girls had been too proud to speak before but were too smart not to speak now.

Petula grabbed Virginia's hand and held it tightly on her lap. She had never experienced such a bonding moment with anyone in her life before, especially a fellow female. Girls were always competition for Petula, people whom she had to outdo and outshine.

Virginia was alarmed at first. She thought she wanted to be told that everything was all in her head, but instead, she found Petula's honesty comforting. There was no point being

in denial. They were alone in a room wearing hospital gowns, waiting for someone they didn't even know to arrive eventually, if ever.

"Don't worry," Petula said, pulling Virginia close. "I won't let anything happen to you."

"Promise?"

This was also probably the first time Petula ever felt truly needed, as opposed to wanted, and she took the responsibility seriously. Feeling protective toward anyone was foreign to her, but she was surprised at how naturally it came to her under the circumstances.

"I promise," Petula swore.

❧

The Wendys were killing time, reading through Petula's chart, texting each other across the room, and hoping not to get busted. Wendy Anderson kept peeling the backs of her sweaty thighs off the vinyl mattress, checking them for signs of cellulite. They'd promised Damen they'd stay in Petula's room and cover for him until he got back, but the real reason they stayed was to check out Dr. Kaufman. A shot at a hot young doctor was the only thing more appealing than Homecoming to them, and Damen worked it like a pro. They were still a little pissed about getting left behind, their dreams of filling Petula's shoes now dashed for good.

"Petula Kensington and Damen Dylan," Wendy Anderson trumpeted snidely. "Together again!"

"Not exactly," Wendy Thomas laughed. "More like 'Damen and the Real Girl.'"

"Could you imagine if skullface over there knew what was going on?" Wendy Anderson said, pointing to Scarlet.

"Can anyone say *hostage situation*?"

Before the girls could finish laughing at their own jokes, they heard someone approaching. It was Dr. Kaufman, making his afternoon rounds.

"Get in bed," Wendy Thomas shrieked urgently. "Someone's coming. . . ."

Wendy Thomas paused and pondered what she'd just said. "Bet you've heard *that* before!"

Wendy Anderson wrapped her head in a towel to cover her rich, brunette locks, hopped onto the plastic mattress, and crept her middle finger out of the sheet toward Wendy Thomas, afterward proceeding to lie perfectly still. Wendy Thomas headed for the doorway and leaned in it, her taut arms and legs stretched across the entrance like bicycle spokes inside a wheel.

"Hello," she said invitingly to the young doctor as he approached. "Can I help you?"

Damen wasn't kidding about Kaufman, he was definitely worth a cubic zirconium-encrusted tiara or two, and then some. If Wendy Anderson wasn't so afraid to move her hand to pat herself on the back for deciding to stay, she would have.

"I'm here to examine the Kensington girls."

"Why bother?" Wendy asked dismissively. "Aren't they both veggies?"

"Excuse me?"

"I mean, it's really all over except for the funeral, right?" Wendy whispered knowingly to him. "Time for us to move on."

"Where there's life, there's hope, miss. Now if you will excuse me . . ."

Dr. Kaufman began to push his way through the Wendy blockade in the doorway, prying her manicured fingers from the door jamb when his pager went off. He reached for it to check the caller when he got a second urgent page over the hospital intercom.

"Dr. Kaufman, please attend to room three-one-one. Code Blue."

Kaufman bolted without a word, and the trundle of resuscitation equipment and footsteps that followed could be heard from every corridor.

"That was close," Wendy Thomas exhaled, totally indifferent to the suffering going on just down the hall. "A little closer would have been nice, though."

"Can you believe how he just took off like that, without even saying goodbye?" Wendy Anderson said, sitting up slowly and cracking her neck. "I'm gonna die if I have to lie in this bed any longer."

"Yeah, let's get out of here."

❧

Dead Ed was in session when Prue, Pam, and Scarlet arrived. Scarlet knocked gently, and Ms. Pierce invited the visitors in. Scarlet stretched her neck around the doorway and waved, meekly.

"Nice to see you again," Ms. Pierce greeted her sincerely, the relief in her voice in sharp contrast to the concern she'd shown when last they met.

The very fact that Scarlet had come back was potentially a good sign, not just for Scarlet but for the whole class.

"Hi, everybody," Scarlet said, then turned to the teacher and asked, "Can my friends come in too?"

"Of course."

With that, Pam and Prue followed Scarlet through the doorway and into the classroom. A wave of nostalgia hit them instantly as they looked the place up and down and from side to side, checking out the new kids, the teacher, the wall hangings, their old desks. Nothing had changed, except the faces and the fact that the room felt smaller than they'd remembered.

"What are you doing back here?" Paramour Polly sniped, decidedly less happy to see Scarlet and company than her instructor and feeling a little threatened by the older girls with her. The rest of the kids were suspicious and grumbling as well.

"Don't worry. I'm not here to cause any more trouble, but . . ."

"We need to find our friend Charlotte . . . ," Prue said, cutting to the chase.

"Not again," Lipo Lisa interrupted. "Why don't you just Google this chick or put out an Amber Alert or something?"

"Shut up and listen, 'Rexy,'" Prue barked, falling easily back into her Dead Ed leadership role and getting everyone's attention. "We don't have a lot of time."

"Do any of you remember if you came here from the hospital?" Pam asked calmly.

This whole topic was generally taboo for Dead Ed because

of all the raw feelings it tended to bring to the surface. Pam looked over at Ms. Pierce, who nodded her approval for Pam to continue. The teacher understood the gravity of the situation and admired the risks they all had taken for their friend.

"I'm sorry," Pam offered the class, "but it's really important."

"Okay," Scarlet said, "who wants to go first?"

The kids looked around at one another, none willing to put a toe in first. As the seconds ticked by, the expressions on their faces went blank as each of them revisited their ending, a subject that they'd always been encouraged to carefully avoid.

"I came from Hot Bed," Tanning Tilly said, missing the irony, as a look of sadness swept across her face.

"I came from my best friend's boyfriend's house," Paramour Polly said, half prideful and half ashamed, as if she were confessing her sin to a priest.

Scarlet hated bringing them back to the place in time when they'd lost their lives, but Ms. Pierce motioned for her to keep going. This was painful, but it was something they needed to face in order for them to graduate. Ms. Pierce was just hoping that it wasn't all a little premature, seeing that there was still a seat left.

"I ended up at Hawthorne Hospital," Blogging Bianca said.

"You did?" the three girls shouted excitedly in unison.

"Well, I ended up there," Bianca said. "They tried to administer anti-clotting agents intravenously, but I'd been on

the computer so long that by the time I got to the hospital, I was DOA."

"So you didn't die in the hospital?" Scarlet asked dejectedly.

"No, I'm afraid not," Bianca replied apologetically.

"I died at the hospital," Green Gary spoke up unexpectedly from the back of the room.

"Can you take us there?" Prue asked.

Gary looked at Ms. Pierce for permission.

"You can take them, but you will need a pass," the teacher said, removing a big wooden paddle engraved with the Latin motto DUM SPIRO, SPERO from her desk drawer.

"How many trees did it take to make this paddle?" Gary asked, ever true to his greenager roots.

"Not as many as it takes to make a coffin, hummus head," Prue jibed as they hightailed it out of the room.

Chapter 19

The Supernatural and the Superficial

Everybody has a heart.
Except some people.
–Bette Davis

Looks are everything.

There are a few ways of looking at someone.
You can look up to them, you can look down
on them or you can look through them, but
after some serious life lessons, you can learn
to look right at them. Petula was always
looking down and Charlotte was tired of
looking up, but all they really had to do was
look inside themselves and see each other
for who they were.

**harlotte and Maddy hitched a ride on** a freight elevator with Damen and a custodial cart carrying Petula's nearly lifeless body like a sarcophagus down to the ground floor. Besides Petula, the cart was loaded with various cleaning solutions, mops, brooms, rags, paper towels, toilet paper, and garbage bags. Not a very glamorous treasure chest, Charlotte thought, a person of such nobility.

Damen wheeled the cart out of the lift and toward the swinging rear doors of the employee entrance. The cart wasn't designed to carry that much weight, and he could feel the wheels turning in, making it difficult to steer. Nobody thought much about it as they saw the young man in janitor's garb struggling with the heavy load. The hospital was a pretty faceless place for entry level cleaning help, and Damen's struggle hardly attracted any notice at all, except, he imagined, from

his passenger, unconscious in the canvas bag he was wheeling around.

"Sorry, Petula." He winced each time he slammed the wall or bounced over a crack in the basement floor.

"Brutal," Maddy giggled with each jostle of Petula's bobblehead, as she pulled Charlotte along, making sure to keep pace with Damen as he scrambled, like the quarterback he was, into the parking lot.

Damen pushed the cart through the large doors and parked it next to a smelly gray Dumpster while he hastily discarded his janitor's smock and tossed it in the garbage bin. He was relieved to be rid of the disguise, even after such a short while. It wasn't exactly the kind of hero's costume he imagined donning as a boy, but the mission he was undertaking might have proven too much even for a superman. He steered the cart over to his car, looked around, opened the passenger door, gently lifted Petula in, and positioned her in as natural a way as possible.

Maddy and Charlotte hopped in the backseat behind him. Charlotte stared at Petula and remembered being in that passenger seat, playing "he loves me, he loves me not" as she pretended to slide under his arm. She laughed to herself about Petula being just as invisible to him now as she had been then, and if Charlotte hadn't already choked to death on a gummy bear, she'd definitely be choking on irony now.

The slamming of the passenger-side door startled her, and she turned her attention to Damen once again as he jumped into the driver's seat. He fiddled with the rearview mirror for a second, and Charlotte imagined he was looking right at her.

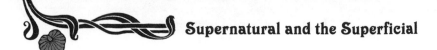

She stared back at him, into those warm, caring eyes she'd never quite gotten over, even after all this time.

৩৩

Gary led Pam, Prue, and Scarlet from Dead Ed back to the hospital in no time at all.

"Hey," Gary called as the girls began to split off from him. "It's this way."

"I just need to check on something first," Scarlet said, walking slowly toward their room.

As they got closer, Pam and Prue noticed Scarlet slowing down until she was practically stopped just a few feet before the doorway.

"What's up?" Pam asked gently.

Scarlet didn't answer. She wasn't sure how to answer. There might be a big difference between what she was hoping to see and what she could reasonably expect.

First off, there was the little matter of her own body lying there. She'd seen goofy pictures of herself asleep, but the thought of watching herself breathe her last breaths was a bit much. And then there was Damen. He might still be all caught up in doting on Petula. She didn't know how she would react if she walked in there and caught him mid-dote, and she'd feel guilty for being jealous of her dying sister.

"Now is not the time for cold feet," Prue warned.

Pam and Prue walked in first, breaking the ice for Scarlet, who followed close behind.

No Damen. That was the first thing Scarlet noticed. She saw his things scattered around, but he was MIA. Home

showering, maybe, she rationalized. Although she was a little hurt at having been abandoned, she was also a little relieved not to find him wringing his hands over Petula instead of her.

"Ugh," Scarlet sighed as she walked over to her own limp form.

This was exactly what she was afraid of. She even looked pale to herself, more so than usual, and frail. The IV drip in her arm made her wince, and the heart monitor beeping irritated her like one of those "mosquito" dispersal sirens that supposedly only teens can hear. She could see the outline of her legs beneath the heavily starched white sheets, which clung to her knees and feet like some sort of poly/cotton shroud. It was odd and not much fun to have the experience of totally being able to see yourself as others see you.

Pam, Prue, and Gary, not wanting to intrude on Scarlet's privacy, snuck behind Petula's curtained side of the room to check on things. Scarlet was shocked back into reality by an audible gasp from her three friends.

"She's gone!" Pam shouted from behind the curtain on the other side of the semi-private room.

"No!" Scarlet shrieked, a flood of emotion nearly drowning her. "She can't be . . . dead!"

"No," Prue clarified, grabbing Scarlet by the shoulders. "I mean she's really gone."

"As in *not here*," Gary confirmed, pulling away Petula's privacy drapes and revealing the empty bed, stuffed with towels and pillows.

"Where the hell can she be?" Prue spat.

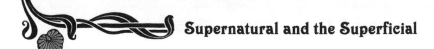
"That's one possibility," Gary butted in sarcastically.

"This is bad news," Pam advised. "Without her body, it doesn't matter whether we find her soul or not."

"What if they, you know, took her body," Scarlet asked nervously, fishing for an answer she really didn't want to hear.

"Who's *they*?" Prue asked firmly, not wanting to say what was just then crossing all their minds. Did Scarlet mean the medical examiner or did she think that Charlotte may have taken her sister's body for a more permanent spin with Maddy's help? It wasn't entirely clear to any of them which might be worse.

"Pam, you go down to the morgue and see if she's there," Prue ordered, choosing not to overdo the kidnapping scenario just yet.

"I'm not going down there!" Pam said sheepishly.

Just then Prue noticed a visible trace of Petula, her hospital gown lying crumpled on the floor. She started gathering clues. She noticed that Petula's chart was still clipped to the bed. It hadn't been closed out, which meant Petula hadn't been discharged or died. Finally, she picked up her hair extensions on the night table. She showed Scarlet the evidence.

"Wait, they wouldn't have left this stuff behind if she was gone," Prue asked. "Would they?"

Scarlet walked over to Petula's side of the room and inspected it. The area around her bed looked a lot like her bedroom after a series of pre-date quick changes. She noticed the faint imprint of an unfamiliar shade of foundation and eye shadow on her pillow and caught a whiff of the barest scent of a really wretched fragrance that could only belong to one person — or more like two.

Then Scarlet noticed the most important clue of all. Petula's Homecoming dress was missing too. Either Petula was already dead and buried in it, or . . .

"The Wendys," Scarlet said out loud. "They've got her."

"What for?" Pam asked, giving Scarlet a reality check. "She's barely alive."

"Where would they take her anyway?" Prue added.

"Homecoming," she said assuredly, holding up remnants of a formal quick-change.

How could Damen allow that, Scarlet wondered. Unless . . . he was with her. Immediately Scarlet's heart sank to her stomach. She would rather have faced her lifeless body than face the fact that Damen, who said he wouldn't leave her side under any conditions, might be with Petula.

❧

As Damen raced to Hawthorne High, Petula swung from one side to the other like a broken pendulum, her mouth slightly agape, with each sharp turn of the steering wheel. This wasn't the first time she'd been in that condition in his car, Damen recalled, but this was definitely different. He looked over at her, bouncing aimlessly like a crash test dummy, and realized he hadn't been that close to her in a very long time, nor had he wanted to be. Though Petula was in the seat next to him, it was Scarlet he had on his mind.

Damen had texted ahead to the football coach and word was spreading like impetigo that he was on his way — with Petula. Kids began drawing up oversized signs and messages of support. PETULA'S TOE-TALLY COOL and SHE HAS RISEN

banners were painted on bed sheets and hung from the bleachers. The emcee began rewriting his coronation speech, and cheerleaders retooled their Petula chants abandoned after she took ill.

"Whether she's alive or not, Petula Kensington is so damn hot!" was quickly replaced by a new one, *"O-M-G-W-T-F,"* they spelled aloud, cheering: *"Petula's toe is all healed up!"* which rang from the stands so loudly Damen could almost hear it as they drove up to the school.

Most everybody was thrilled to hear the news, except for returning alumni Petula-haters and the other would-be Homecoming queens who had been grasping for votes all year as well. With Petula out of the contest, it was anybody's game. Her return, however, would mean certain defeat for the other girls, especially given all the bonus sympathy she'd receive for overcoming death and everything.

As Damen and Petula arrived, the gate to the school parking lot opened, just as it always had for Hawthorne's First Couple. Damen rolled by the checkpoint and gave the guard the thumbs-up.

"Long time," the old acquaintance said fondly to Damen. "Glad to see you're back."

"Good to be back," Damen said, flashing a big smile and heading onward.

It wasn't really, but this was just the littlest of the frauds Damen was perpetrating at that moment. He would have said anything to keep Petula from attracting attention. Lucky for him she was generally so rude to people they knew better than to greet her or look her in the eye for that matter. He never

thought he would ever appreciate her condescending nature as much as he did now.

Damen pulled into a reserved space at the head of the red carpet. The less walking, the better. He got out and waved at the crowd of photographers anxiously awaiting his arrival. He stepped around his car, obscuring their view of Petula as much as possible, and gently lifted her out, making sure that her head was leaning against his shoulder for support. He turned, holding Petula in his arms like a bride about to be carried over the threshold, and stood for a few seconds as flashes popped around him and the bystanders roared their approval.

"Can you believe this?" Maddy said, rubbing all the adoration for the Petula-and-Damen display in Charlotte's nose. "How cool to be them?"

"Yeah," Charlotte agreed. "Cool."

Petula's huge toothy grin and bug eyes were a very uncharacteristic show of emotion, the photo hounds commented, but then this was a very special day for her. A very special reunion, not just with Damen but with her status at Hawthorne as well. Damen, on the other hand, was hoping for a reunion of his own.

"Remember," Damen muttered to himself, realizing these pictures would be incriminating if he was successful in bringing Scarlet back. "It's all for you."

"Did you hear that?" Maddy nudged, misinterpreting Damen's intentions yet again. "He's totally ditching your friend for her comatose sister."

Charlotte looked dumbfounded. This was really happening. Damen and Petula back together again, hogging the limelight,

soaking up the praise, just like always, and Charlotte, she was sidelined, totally invisible, just like always.

Everyone was shouting questions and Damen could barely think. He was hoping this first big blast of admiration would start to bring her around, but she didn't move a muscle. One thing he was sure of was that he could not stick around here. He had to keep moving.

"No interviews, please," Damen yelled as he bolted down the carpet into the secure area where the Homecoming parade floats were tanked.

∞

The office was feeling colder than a meat locker now, and Petula reached her arm around Virginia's small shoulder, pulling her in close to her body. Such an unselfish act was so alien to Petula that she wasn't even sure how hard to squeeze. Virginia made it a moot point as she nestled comfortably into Petula's electrolysized armpit, looked up at her, and smiled. The girl was much less afraid all of a sudden.

"You look sad," Virginia said.

"I just want to go to Homecoming so badly. This is my year."

"How do you know?" the girl asked sarcastically, flashing her beauty queen savvy and quick wit once again. "Did someone do the judge?"

Petula didn't answer but squeezed her as tightly as she could, affectionately, prompting the little girl to giggle for the first time since she got there.

Chapter 20

Divine Comedy

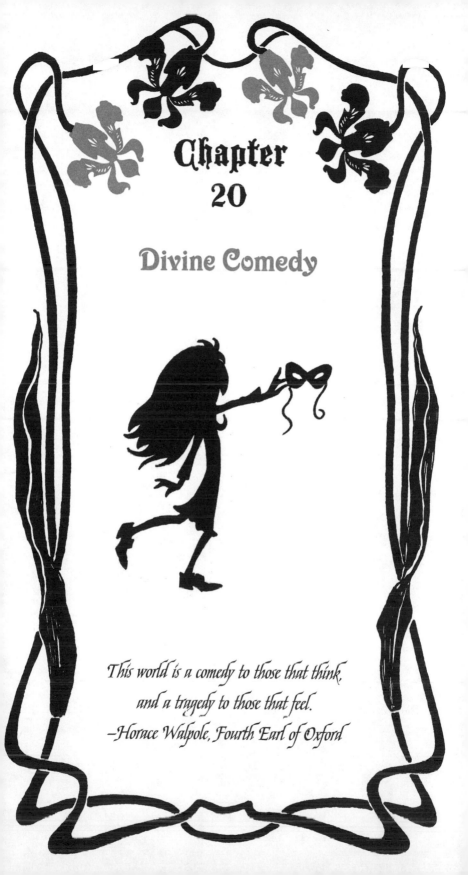

This world is a comedy to those that think,
and a tragedy to those that feel.
—Horace Walpole, Fourth Earl of Oxford

Better she than me.

They say comedy is tragedy happening to
someone else. We try to find the funny in
the misfortune of others mostly as a defense
mechanism, but there is a limit. Death is
no laughing matter. With everything she'd
ever wanted and had so reluctantly given up
being paraded right in front of her again,
Charlotte began to feel like everything was
one big cosmic joke—on her.

he Wendys tiptoed down the hospital corridor looking for the fastest, least obvious, exit. Traipsing around in their tight suits and heels was not exactly the most unobstrusive means of transport, but they had no options. They needed to get out of the hospital and to the high school pronto, so hiding in plain sight seemed a wise strategy.

"Damen is going to be so pissed," Wendy Thomas whispered.

"So what? I'm not missing Homecoming for him."

"Yeah, he didn't think twice about leaving the Living Dead Doll all alone back there anyway."

Just then, the grief-stricken young couple Damen had seen earlier spilled out of another room down the hall, the mother clutching a beautiful ribbon, which fell to the floor unnoticed in her distress. As the woman wept convulsively, hugging her husband and hanging on to him for support, the desk nurse pointed them toward the chapel.

"We are praying for her," the head nurse said, offering whatever comfort she could. "I'm sorry."

"Me too," Wendy Anderson said sympathetically as she eavesdropped.

"How sweet," Wendy Thomas added with uncharacteristic sincerity.

The girls, done congratulating themselves for the momentary show of compassion, returned to more pressing matters.

"The ribbon," Wendy Anderson observed enviously. "It shouldn't be on the floor like that."

"No, it shouldn't," Wendy Thomas agreed.

"It'll go perfectly with my outfit" Wendy Anderson continued. "That blue will really make my eyes pop."

The Wendys eyed the ribbon, gave it some thought, and decided it would be difficult to steal. A triage room at Hawthorne Hospital was not, after all, the change stalls at Bloomingdale's. But, as the distraught couple slowly made their way down the hall toward the chapel, the Wendys made their move.

"One girl's trash," Wendy Anderson began.

"Is another's vintage accessory," Wendy Thomas concluded, hooking the prize with her pointed-toed shoe and tossing it in the air toward Wendy Anderson's expert grasp, honed at many a downtown sample sale.

❧

The Homecoming candidates were beginning to take their places in their floats as mothers from Hawthorne's alumni and their young daughters stood behind barricades to hopefully get pictures of their budding queens with a member of the royal court. The "floats" were actually cars decked out in papier mâché sculptures, dyed toilet paper streamers, and cardboard,

but the Hawthorne student body and returning alums had no trouble suspending disbelief. It was their very own Tournament of Roses parade, even if less imaginative eyes saw only a ridiculous kind of trailer park soapbox derby come to life.

The "techer" candidate, a hair technology major, made over her Pinto in the shape of a hair dryer. It was a given every year that all the "techers" would rally behind one of their own, despite the odds, and try to vote her into the Homecoming court. They were used to coming in last, so just being there was an annual triumph for them.

Then there was the skanky candidate whose float was better suited to a window display at the local Victoria's Secret. To no one's surprise, her date was Josh Valence. He and his alma mater were despised at Hawthorne, which didn't matter a bit to him. He was always willing to grandstand in front of a crowd, even one that hated him.

Damen glared nastily over at the couple, especially Josh. This whole thing with Petula was really his fault. *Who dumps a sick girl on her driveway and takes off,* Damen thought. Petula was rarely deserving of any sympathy, but Josh made her seem like Mother Teresa.

The Wendys had no floats, just sleek matching candy-apple red, open-top sports cars, which sat vacant for the moment. They were surprisingly tasteful, but the vehicles were so much the same, you could only surmise they were intentionally planning to split the vote, thus guaranteeing Petula the top spot in the final tally anyway.

Petula opted for the subdued approach as well, except for the blazing pink color of her Corvette. She never wanted to be

overshadowed by anything or anyone, even her own parade float, and the shade of the car paint had been meticulously co-ordinated with her dress.

Damen lifted Petula onto the backseat of the convertible and sat up next to her, smiling for the crowd, supporting her like a ventriloquist with his dummy. He gripped her elbow and lifted it, waving her arm back and forth. He began to sweat a little as real fear began to seep through the phony grin he had plastered on his face.

What if Petula actually died on the field? He would be responsible and would probably be charged with kidnapping and murder. Second-degree at least. Open and shut. The Wendys could certainly be counted on to cut a deal and testify against him, although, he thought, they would probably have enjoyed being called "accessories" in the newspaper. He would lose everything — his freedom, his future, and most impor-tantly, Scarlet.

He imagined being featured on one of those Dateline spe-cials where they profile criminals, prompting viewers to ask their television sets — *What kind of person would do a thing like that?* Despite the bout of self-recrimination, there was no turn-ing back now. He signaled to his driver that they were ready, and the procession began. Petula's car was last in the lineup.

Charlotte and Maddy jumped in the backseat and looked up at the couple.

"Why don't you hop up there with them?" Maddy sug-gested. "Look at all these people."

Charlotte had never seen Maddy so giddy, which was sur-prising since she didn't find Maddy to be much of a people

person or the sentimental type who would get off on a Home-coming parade.

"That might be fun," Charlotte said, trying in vain to hide her eagerness. Sitting on top of the backseat with them, it was a whole new experience. The screams from the crowd, the souped-up engines roaring, horns beeping, the music blaring was all so much louder, so much more vivid. It was thrilling.

Damen proceeded to wave Petula's arm in that generic kind of crowd-pleasing way and pasted a big perma-smile on his face. As the cars circled, Charlotte was overwhelmed by the cheers and accolades thrust from the bleachers. She didn't need to imagine what it would be like to be in that car, next to Damen. She was there. Now.

Charlotte could barely hear the voice of her own conscience any longer. The only voice that seemed to break through the crowd noise was Maddy's.

"It's so amazing what he's doing for her. He must really love her."

"He did once," Charlotte affirmed. "But I thought that was over."

"You can put a stop to this, Charlotte. You can bring Petula *and* yourself back."

Each girl was announced over the loudspeaker to polite applause as their car approached the stands, but the crowd erupted as Petula's car came around the front of the bleachers. Charlotte bathed in the spotlight as Petula was introduced, her mini-bio — one Petula had clearly written herself especially for the occasion — read over the PA system:

PETULA KENSINGTON IS A RETURNING SENIOR AT
HAWTHORNE HIGH.

LIKES: CHIHUAHUAS, BRAZILIAN WAXES, AND VEGGIE BUR-
GERS ON FIFTEEN-GRAIN LOW-CARB BREAD.

DISLIKES: NEGATIVITY AND THE COLORS BROWN AND BLACK,
ESPECIALLY WHEN WORN TOGETHER.

SHE IS THE ACTING CAPTAIN OF THE CHEERLEADING SQUAD,
WHICH UNDER HER LEADERSHIP WON THE PRESTIGIOUS TRI-
STATE SPIRIT AWARD. SHE HAS ALSO COMPLETED A FULL YEAR
OF COMMUNITY SERVICE WITH GRACE AND DIGNITY, ROLLING
UP HER THREE-QUARTER SLEEVES AND HELPING HER FELLOW
MAN BY SERVING COFFEE AND BUSING TABLES. SHE CHANGED
THE WAY VOLUNTEERS ARE REGARDED, STAMPING OUT PREJU-
DICE ONE CUP AT A TIME. ADDITIONALLY, SHE HAS LOBBIED
THE LOCAL CORRECTIONS DEPARTMENT FOR MORE FASHION-
ABLE PRISON WEAR, COMMUNITY SERVICE ATTIRE, AND AC-
CESSORIES. MS. KENSINGTON PLANS ON USING THE CROWN
AND HER TITLE TO RESTORE HOPE TO THE COMMUNITY AS
WELL AS TO LAUNCH HER OWN CLOTHING LINE AND, IF THAT
IS SUCCESSFUL, DOLLS IN HER LIKENESS.

All of Petula's adoring fans were yelling at fever pitch,
drowning out the techer and skank contingents as expected,
and Charlotte was finding it just as hard to control herself. This
was the kind of moment that Petula lived for, planned for. The
kind of moment so powerful, so insanely ego-gratifying, that

it could drag a dying girl back from the edge of the abyss, and hopefully, Damen was betting, bring her sister back with her.

"It's now or never," Damen yelled in Petula's ear, loudly enough for both Maddy and Charlotte to hear.

Everything Charlotte had ever wanted was literally within her reach. Charlotte's eyes met Maddy's and she saw a gleam, a glee, and a scary delight in them that she'd never seen before.

"This is your time, Charlotte," Maddy pushed even more forcefully. "You heard him, it's now or never."

Charlotte looked over at Damen and Petula and back to Maddy, hopelessly confused.

"But what about Scarlet?" Charlotte asked weakly.

"You'll be doing them all a favor," Maddy went on. "Do it. Now!"

The applause, the cheers, the revving car motors, the lights, the signs all seemed to agree with Maddy. The crowd wanted Petula back, Scarlet wanted Petula back, and from the looks of things, even Damen wanted Petula back. And she was the only one who could make it happen.

She reached slowly for Petula and placed her hand near her heart.

☙❧

"Charlotte," a desperate voice called out from across the field.

"Scarlet!" Charlotte yelled back, shocked by the sight of her friend rushing toward her.

Charlotte wasn't sure if Scarlet was upset with her or Damen at first, but the closer she got, with Pam and Prue at her side, the clearer it became.

"What are you doing?" she screamed.

The horror on Scarlet's face and the disappointment on Prue's and Pam's faces were almost too much to bear. Charlotte was speechless. Maddy, unflustered by the gang approaching, jumped to Charlotte's defense.

"Maybe you should be minding your own business a little more," Maddy warned, pointing to Damen's hand around Petula's waist.

Scarlet did glance up and was none too thrilled to see Damen so close to Petula.

"This . . . is not what it looks like," Charlotte stammered. "I'm not a body whore."

"That's right," Prue jumped in, explaining to Scarlet. "Charlotte's not."

"She is," Pam turned and pointed accusingly at Maddy.

Maddy just smiled as the other girls glowered at her. Charlotte said nothing.

"Good luck proving that one," Maddy laughed. "I wasn't the one sitting up there, landsharking Petula to get Damen."

"But you told me to," Charlotte said to Maddy. "I was only going to do it to help. . . ."

Charlotte sounded unconvincing to the crew around her because she wasn't sure herself what her motives really were anymore.

"I just wanted to do the right thing," Charlotte babbled.

"For who?" Scarlet chided. "Me or you?"

"She didn't come knocking on *your* door," Maddy said, playing both sides.

"Don't give me that," Scarlet countered, scanning the field. "She wanted all . . . this."

"Not so fast," Pam interrupted. "Maddy's been plotting this all along."

"Bull," Maddy argued defensively. "Charlotte's a big girl. Don't blame me for her decisions."

But Pam wasn't just speculating. She motioned to Prue that it was time to say what they knew.

"I got a call," Prue said snidely to Maddy, "from an acquaintance of yours right after Charlotte called in sick."

Charlotte shrugged her shoulders a little, silently acknowledging the ridiculousness of a dead girl using a sick day.

"The call was from an up-and-coming young starlet almost suicidal from guilt," Pam picked up, "because her friend, 'Matilda,' died mysteriously while they were both competing for a break-out role."

"Apparently, Maddy, as she was called, was a forgotten former child star living in Las Vegas . . . ," Prue continued.

"Sin City," Scarlet noted.

"And she was desperate to land this role," Pam said, "to make her big comeback."

"Comeback from where?" Scarlet bit. "I've never heard of her."

"She convinced her friend they needed some underarm Botox shots, which she'd gotten on the black market," Prue explained. "So their sweaty pit stains wouldn't show on camera during the audition."

"Tested on actresses, never on animals," Scarlet said dramatically.

"Anyway, within hours of giving each other the shots," Prue said, "Maddy came down with all the symptoms of botulism. Dry mouth, blurred vision, trouble breathing, muscle weakness. The whole deal."

"Did the friend say if she crapped herself?" Scarlet asked, rankling Maddy. "I hear that happens too."

"She was hospitalized and missed the audition, obviously, and her friend got the role." Prue concluded. "Maddy died two days later from complications."

"I don't get it," Charlotte asked, probing Prue for more information. "What did Maddy do wrong?"

"Her friend didn't believe it," Prue said, "but the police determined that the overdose injection was meant for her, not Maddy. The Wacktress mixed them up and saved her own life in the process."

"Must have been a *killer* role they were fighting for," Scarlet opined snidely.

Even in the huge, open outdoor space, Maddy felt her world closing in on her.

"Dying like that," Prue added, "follows you forever."

"She needed to corrupt someone else," Pam said. "So she could . . ."

"Go to Hell!" Maddy said as if she just power-gargled with gravel.

"Exactly," Prue said. "It is the only way for her to advance in *her* world."

Charlotte kept her cool and listened impassively to the gossiping ghosts, processing the reveal taking place.

As they rolled slowly toward the reviewing stand like some

kind of supernatural clown car, Charlotte stared over at Scarlet, who was fixated on Damen, who was gripping both Petula and the headrest of the Corvette, preparing manically for he didn't quite know what. Charlotte could almost see the time ticking away as Scarlet's and Damen's pupils both widened, bigger and bigger, in response to the growing mania of the crowd and their own increasing desperation. She'd heard enough. It was time for her to come clean too. The calmness of spirit and peace of mind she'd achieved at Fall Ball last year returned to her, and Pam, as usual, was the first to notice her change in demeanor.

"You don't look very surprised, Charlotte?" Pam asked quizzically.

"I'm not," Charlotte said, shocking the girls around her, including Maddy. "I've suspected it from the beginning."

Maddy lowered her eyes, shamed not so much at being outed as the underminer she was but at her own defeat by someone she considered so pathetic. She'd underestimated Charlotte, taking her for an easy mark.

"Why didn't you say something?" Pam asked. "We could have gotten rid of her."

"Keep your friends close," Charlotte instructed, "but your enemies closer."

"Gangsta," Scarlet mumbled, approvingly. "You wanted to know what she was up to before you made a move."

"Before Scarlet came, I was the only one in danger from her," Charlotte explained. "But once she offered to come to Hawthorne, I knew Maddy wanted to take us all down."

"She planned the whole thing?" Scarlet asked.

"Not exactly," Charlotte explained. "At first, getting to me was enough. But the call Maddy took for me was from Scarlet," Charlotte continued. "When she figured out what Scarlet was planning to do to save Petula, she saw a much bigger opportunity."

"She figured Scarlet would get stuck in Dead Ed trying to cross over," Pam nodded, everything making sense now. "Filling a seat not meant for her."

"She would have stopped them *all* from being able to cross over," Prue concurred, "taken that whole class out and kept her from reaching you."

"But when Scarlet actually showed up," Charlotte continued, "it changed her plan."

"She offered to help," Pam said, "because by convincing you to bring Petula back, she could have damned not just your soul, offing Petula's and Scarlet too."

"I got greedy," Maddy said offhandedly. "Sue me."

"You saved our lives," Scarlet said solemnly, Charlotte's sacrifice just beginning to sink in. "And more."

"Wait, so you called in sick to signal us to come find you?" Pam said, putting all the pieces together.

Charlotte smiled acknowledging Pam's theory.

"And you knew that whichever way Maddy suggested we go, I'd go the opposite," Scarlet said.

"Yeah, I was relying on your Oppositional Defiance Disorder," Charlotte chuckled.

"So it was all an act?" Prue asked. "Moping around, possessing Petula."

"Not entirely," Charlotte explained honestly and a little

ashamed. "Just because I knew what Maddy was up to doesn't mean I wasn't tempted. She offered me everything I missed, everything I wanted. It was hard to resist . . . and I almost didn't."

"I was just doing my job," Maddy croaked to Charlotte. "Don't take it personally."

"That's what people say after they screw you over," Scarlet rebutted.

"What's so great about doing good anyway?" Maddy propositioned. "What did it get any of you? A telemarketing job?"

"Some people say good deed is its own reward," Charlotte responded, her moral compass totally reset and working overtime at the moment.

"And the road to Hell," Maddy spouted, "is paved with good intentions."

"Drop me a postcard when you get there," Prue quipped.

Maddy didn't see any reason to stick around much longer. She may have lost round one, but the battle was far from over, and she'd have other chances to earn her horns. She eyed Damen and Petula on the trunk of the Corvette, winked snidely at Scarlet, and made her move.

"If Charlotte doesn't want a comeback," Maddy exploded, "I do." Maddy thrust herself into Petula's body and brought her to life as if she'd just been shocked by a 10,000-volt defibrillator.

"Stop her!" Pam and Prue screamed helplessly as Maddy slipped their grasp, but it was too late. This didn't need to be consensual.

Petula's body rose slowly from her seat into a standing

position and raised her arms triumphantly to a massive roar from the crowd.

"I'm back!" Petula shouted, uttering her and Maddy's innermost feelings.

Damen jumped up and roared, too, his scheme appearing to pay off at last. A second later, he thought it might be paying off a little too well, as Petula reached for his face, opened her mouth wide, and pulled him close for a sloppy wet kiss.

"No, Petula!" Damen shouted, struggling to keep her at bay as her tongue flicked the air in front of him.

The crowd roared even louder in anticipation. This was much more than they could have ever bargained for.

Even with all his strength, Damen could barely hold Petula back. It was like she was possessed or something. Scarlet was freaking.

"Charlotte," Scarlet screamed, "please, do something!"

Before she could think about it, Charlotte zipped inside Petula, just before the liplock, and broke it up. The first time she'd tried to get inside her, they were in a car as well, she recalled, but this was not Driver's Ed. As Markov so rightly said, "Now is not then." Inhabiting Petula was everything she'd imagined, putting Charlotte on sensory overload. It was like being in the priciest department store ever with an unlimited charge account. Everything was available. Anything seemed possible.

The screaming crowd, the camera flashes, the chants and cheers, the flat belly, the perfect boobs, the toned legs, the hard butt, the fit of the dress along Petula's taut body, all felt

like blaring music pumping from the DJ booth in an empty club. It was dizzying, addictive, saturating, as if Petula's being itself fed on the approval and the excitement. The world really was different through Petula's eyes. Damen was right — if anything could bring her around, it was Homecoming.

It turned out the most exciting thing of all was not inside of Petula, but outside of her. It was Damen's touch. She could feel his warm hands on Petula's shoulder and forearm, holding her tightly, forcefully in the car seat. It had been a long while since she'd felt him, and feeling him now reminded her of just how long it had been. As Charlotte continued to feel with Petula's skin, see with her eyes, hear with her ears, Maddy's obnoxious giggle somehow broke through. Charlotte turned around to face her. In a weird way, Maddy had gotten what she'd been after, hadn't she? Charlotte thought. Maddy had lured her in. Charlotte had taken over Petula.

"How does it feel to be one of the beautiful people?" Maddy asked seductively.

Silently, Charlotte approached Maddy, as if she were about to embrace her in gratitude.

"That's one role you'll never have to worry about playing," Charlotte whispered in her ear as she struggled to overpower her traitorous roomie, holding on for dear life — Petula's and Scarlet's both.

As the car cruised around the track toward the winner's circle, Petula's entire body was tossed, forward and back, by Charlotte and Maddy's faceoff. To the mesmerized crowd, it appeared as if Petula was headbanging to the music, and they all began to follow suit. Soon the bleachers were a sea of

bopping heads and rock horns, that was until Charlotte kicked Maddy out like an underage drinker at the LCB Christmas party.

"You're out!" Charlotte yelled as she gave Maddy the boot.

Suddenly, Petula went limp. Damen, surprised, caught her before she hit the trunk of the car. Maddy evacuated Petula and Charlotte followed, chasing her away.

"Later, Lose-ifer," Scarlet mocked.

"I'll be seeing you," Maddy said ominously as she exited into the crowd.

Charlotte got high fives from Pam and Prue and a big hug from Scarlet.

"What happened in there?" Scarlet asked.

"You don't want to know," Charlotte said.

"Well, I know you kicked her crazy, has-been self outta here," Scarlet crowed, proud of her friend once again.

"And you thought I was a bitch!" Prue joked, getting more groans than giggles from her ghostly gal pals.

Once the laughter subsided, Scarlet looked at Charlotte and felt it was time to mend fences.

"I'm sorry I doubted you."

"Don't be sorry," Charlotte said, honestly. "I don't really know what I would have done if you guys hadn't shown up when you did."

Scarlet understood Charlotte's doubts.

"Besides," Charlotte modestly reminded her, "Damen is really the one you need to thank. He knew the way back for you was through Petula. He tried to bring her back too, but mostly for your sake."

Not to mention, Scarlet thought, he had held off Maddy *and* Petula from that kiss. No small feat.

"He must really care for you," Pam added.

It meant so much to Scarlet that the girls were supporting her, pumping her up. Before she had a chance to ponder it any further, however, Petula's ankle monitor went off.

Damen was panicked but wouldn't leave. He'd almost brought her all the way back and the only trick he had left up his sleeve was the crowning. If that wouldn't work, she was good as dead anyway.

"We are staying here if it kills me," Damen said as the ankle bracelet continued to monitor Petula's own life slipping further and further away. "Or you."

Suddenly the Wendys showed up in their hot rods, racing toward Petula. They pulled up alongside her car and realized things were not looking good for her.

"Give me that," Damen ordered, pointing to the ribbon around Wendy Anderson's neck.

Without thinking, she tossed it to him and he tied it around Petula's ankle monitor to muffle the relentless beeping that felt like a countdown to a very unhappy ending.

"Asshole!" Wendy screamed, realizing that Petula would always get whatever she wanted, conscious or not.

The ribbon held tight for a while and then flew out of the car onto the ground.

"Hurry," Scarlet yelled urgently, realizing the urgency of the situation. "We have to find Petula's spirit right now."

Charlotte picked up the ribbon and kept it as a memento of one unforgettable night.

Chapter 21

We Will Become Silhouettes

I've seen you laugh at nothing at all
I've seen you sadly weeping
The sweetest thing I ever saw
Was you asleep and dreaming
The Magnetic Fields

You can only feel unloved if you've been loved.

———— ⋅•≻◆≺•⋅ ————

Once you have loved, your soul can never forget it, even if your mind does. Love becomes part of your DNA, your essence. It is as much knowledge as feeling, possessed by the deepest part of your heart and soul. This can be a blessing and a curse. There is no way to fill the emptiness, no treatment for the persistent pain of love that's gone missing, except its return.

ary was waiting outside Scarlet's room when Charlotte, Scarlet, Pam, and Prue arrived.

"Where have you guys been?" he asked frantically. "I have to get back."

"Thanks for waiting," Scarlet said, "and for keeping an eye on me. You really recycled my faith."

Gary chuckled and noticed a stranger in the pack.

"You must be the Famous Charlotte."

Charlotte nodded. She liked that moniker quite a bit.

"I've heard a lot about you and your classmates," Charlotte said. "Thanks for your help."

"Did you find the intake office?" Prue asked.

"Yep," Gary replied. "Ready when you are."

Scarlet peeked into the room and took a look at herself. She looked bad. It wasn't just Petula who was running out of time.

"Ready," she said as they all followed Gary downstairs.

As they walked, Charlotte and Scarlet had a chance to talk, smooth things over, even though it seemed all was already forgiven.

"I wasn't being completely honest with you at Homecoming," Charlotte admitted.

"What do you mean?" Scarlet asked.

"I mean, I did sense Maddy was trouble from the beginning," Charlotte said, "but she still tapped into something that was happening inside of me. Seeing Damen again, watching Petula at Homecoming, another few minutes, and I might really have gone all the way."

"All that matters to me is that when the time came to do the right thing or the wrong thing," Scarlet assured her, "you did what was right."

"I guess," Charlotte answered. "But it's more than just that."

"I'm listening."

Charlotte was talking to herself as much as she was to Scarlet now.

"I've been trying to come to terms with the fact that I'll be trapped here," Charlotte said, feeling a bit sorry for herself. "The phone bank, apartment, bunk beds, lights, elevators, they are still just little illusions of the past, shadows of reality, created to keep us oriented. We don't talk about it, but we all know it."

Scarlet closed her eyes for a moment, both sympathizing with Charlotte's predicament and feeling guilty that she was able to return home, back to her life.

"I'll never go to college, fall in love, or get married, Scarlet," she continued musing in a contemplative tone.

"If anyone could find a way to fall in love over here, it's you," Scarlet said.

Charlotte forced a little smile.

"Look at it this way," Scarlet said, lightening things for a second. "You'll never have to pay rent, get divorced, or go through menopause either."

Charlotte laughed. She could always count on Scarlet to spot the dark cloud.

They stopped walking and continued to talk, looking directly in each other's eyes.

"Maybe that's why I don't get any calls at the phone bank," she added. "I can barely keep myself together, let alone help someone else."

"I know what you mean," Scarlet said, thinking back on what she'd just done for her boyfriend's sake.

"I guess I've accepted losing everything," Charlotte said. "But I don't know that I can let go of you again."

"Maybe you shouldn't," Scarlet said. "I know I won't let go of you."

Charlotte knew that she meant it. They had different lives now — actually, they always had different lives, but the forces that drew them together were even more powerful than the forces that kept them apart.

୭୬

Petula and Virginia had been telling stories and laughing, passing time so easily that they'd almost forgotten they were still waiting to leave. The fun and games were broken up by a trampling sound coming, yet again, from down the hall.

"I hear footsteps again," Virginia said excitedly. "Maybe it's finally time to go."

Petula heard them too, but it sounded more like a mini-stampede than a nurse.

"Maybe," Petula said anxiously.

With that, the footsteps got closer and closer until they could be heard right outside the door.

"This is it," Petula said quietly, holding Virginia's hand tightly.

"This is it," Gary said, grabbing the doorknob and giving it a turn.

The door swung open like it had been bashed by a SWAT team.

"What the . . ." Petula shrieked as she saw a gang of strangers and then her sister blaze in.

"Petula," Scarlet shouted with a feeling of joy and happiness she had not felt at the sight of her sister since they were kids.

"Scarlet," Petula yelled with equal enthusiasm.

The sisters ran toward each other and just as they were about to grab each other in a giant clinch, they hesitated, circling each other with their arms in an air hug.

"Took you long enough," Petula griped, then looked over and saw Charlotte.

"I know you," she said cautiously. "You're that girl that died at school and then got me held back."

"Charlotte," Charlotte said gently.

She was flattered for a second that Petula had remembered her at all. Even now, her acknowledgment meant something.

"But if you're here," Petula reasoned, pointing to Charlotte. "Then I must be dead."

"Not quite," Scarlet said, looking at her sympathetically. "But . . ."

"Almost," Charlotte chimed in.

"We're here to take you back," Scarlet explained.

"Back where?"

"Back to your life," Scarlet said with sincerity. "Back to everyone you love and to everyone who . . . loves you."

Virginia had been standing in the back of the room near the empty desk, taking it all in. She had grown to care about Petula too, in her own way, and she was glad to see her safe now.

"Who are you?" Scarlet asked the young girl.

"That's on a need-to-know basis."

"I see you've been talking to my sister," Scarlet laughed, noting the attitude.

Petula smiled at Virginia quickly, so no one else would see. She was proud of her protégé and of the impact she'd clearly made in just a short time.

"It's okay," Petula advised, tongue at least half in cheek, "you may cooperate."

"I'm Virginia," she said, walking up to each girl and politely shaking her hand. "Pleased to meet me."

The girls all remarked on how young and beautiful she was, which made Petula a little jealous, but oddly proud, and after the pleasantries were through, Scarlet whispered to Petula that they needed to move along.

"Well, enough small talk," Petula said. "We've got to be going. Virginia, come."

Just then, the rear door of the office opened and a dowdy, old nurse entered and took a seat at the desk. She was carrying a file, which she opened and checked over.

"Virginia Johnson," she said. "Is there a Virginia Johnson here?"

Everyone froze. It took Petula a second, but even she began to figure out what was going on.

"Virginia," Petula insisted. "Come with us."

The girl wanted to run to Petula, but she didn't, instinctively understanding what Petula refused to accept.

"She can't come with us," Pam said mournfully.

"Oh," Petula said, emotion sticking in her voice.

"Petula," Scarlet urged, choking back tears of her own.

"No. No. No. No. No, please," Petula begged. "I'll stay."

Scarlet had never seen such selflessness from Petula. It was moving even to Pam and Prue, who had long ago left their emotions and the pain of grief and loss behind.

"Listen," Prue said gently but firmly to her. "If we don't leave now, you won't have a choice."

"Please, I'm afraid," Virginia sobbed, "I want to go with you."

Petula broke down. Pam and Prue consoled her as she flailed at the cold empty air, trying in vain to reach Virginia.

"Virginia Johnson," the nurse impassively called again.

The girl looked at Petula for guidance, and through her tears, Petula found the strength to compose herself and give Virginia the best advice.

"It's okay," Petula said to her.

"Here," the girl finally answered the nurse's call while her eyes looked to Petula's for reassurance.

"I wish I had some way to comfort her." Petula sniffed. "Something to give her."

Charlotte walked over to Petula, reached in her pocket, and pulled out the ribbon.

"Give her this," Charlotte said. "I think it belongs to her anyway."

"Thank you," Petula said to Charlotte with gratitude, and meant it.

Petula walked over to Virginia and then hugged her like they'd never part.

She took the ribbon out and reached for Virginia's hair, running her hand through it slowly, over and over, finally twisting it into a loose braid and tying it into a perfect knot with the royal blue ribbon.

"You will always be beautiful," Petula said, awarding the girl the greatest praise she could think to invoke.

The two of them embraced again, each trying to be strong for the other.

"I'll always be young too," Virginia joked through her tears.

As Petula chest-heaved, laughing through the tears, Charlotte walked up to them and gestured toward the nurse.

"It's time," Charlotte said.

Everyone watched as Virginia walked over to the desk, filled out her paperwork, and took her tag.

"Where do I go now?" Virginia asked innocently.

Virginia looked Charlotte in the eye and recognized that familiar aching in her.

"I'll show you," she volunteered, nodding to Petula not to worry anymore.

"My friend Charlotte will take really good care of you," Petula said.

Charlotte never imagined she'd live long enough to hear those words drop from Petula's lips, but all good things come to those who wait, she guessed.

"Make sure she gets the star treatment."

"I will," Charlotte promised. "A-List all the way."

"I wish I could stay," Petula said, hugging Virginia one last time.

"A very smart person once told me," Virginia explained, "sometimes you just have to let go."

Petula smiled, waved, and turned her back, walking toward the door with Pam and Prue.

"It's time, Virginia," Pam said. "You're going to be late for class."

"Class?"

"Yes, Virginia, there is an Afterlife," Scarlet said, trying to make her laugh a little.

"But it's not so bad," Charlotte said, throwing an appreciative smile to Scarlet.

Scarlet turned to Pam and Prue.

"How can I thank you both?"

"It's cool," Pam answered. "Just stay on your side of the tracks for a while, okay?"

"See you in your nightmares," Prue teased.

"Not if I see you first," Scarlet joked.

"See *you* at work," Prue added, waving bye to Charlotte.

Time was growing short. Scarlet approached Charlotte to say her own farewell.

"You know," Charlotte said, "I would have never betrayed you, right?"

"Of course."

"The odd thing is," Charlotte observed, "when I was actually inside Petula, fighting off Maddy, I could hear the crowd screaming for her, feel her body, and see the whole thing through her eyes even though it was for just that moment."

"You don't have to justify anything to me."

"But instead of wanting to be her," Charlotte continued, "I was glad to be me. Constantly gawked at, judged, scrutinized by people that you don't even know, all secretly wishing for you to fail," Charlotte added, "was not what I thought it would be. Petula is a strong girl."

"There's a first time for everything," Scarlet said lightheartedly, happy her best friend had found peace and contentment at last. "How do I say goodbye to you again?"

"You don't," Charlotte said. "I know where to find you."

"Is that a promise" — Scarlet grinned — "or a threat?"

The girls hugged and kissed each other firmly on their cheeks, cementing their bond, which had proven stronger than life and now, even stronger than death itself.

Scarlet joined Petula, turned for one last look at Charlotte and Virginia, and stepped outside.

Chapter 22

Everybody Says
I Love You

*Life is not about how many breaths you take,
But about how many moments take your breath away.*
—George Curlin

Easy for you to say.

———◆◆◆———

Talk is cheap. If it wasn't, people might not toss around "I love you" like a marked-down phrase in a sale bin. Being stingy with your feelings, saving it up for a worthwhile moment, should make it all the more meaningful to the person you eventually tell, no matter how long it takes. If you are with the right person, it is an investment worth making. The trouble is, sometimes you can wait so long to hear it that you go broke inside.

nd the winner is . . . Petula Kensington!" the emcee screamed.

Petula's spirit re-entered her body just as
her victory was announced. There was such pandemonium
nobody noticed the change, except Damen, who felt her body
jolt again.

"You're back!" Damen was relieved that he didn't have to
carry a semi-corpse up to claim her crown, but nervous that
Petula might try to plant another wet one on him.

"So are you!" Petula grabbed his arm and continued up to
the front without missing a beat.

"Actually, I'm only here to help you so that Scarlet will come back."

"I just saw her. Somewhere," Petula said. "She's fine."

"I gotta get to the hospital!"

"At least take me up to get my crown. It will only take a second."

Damen laughed, nodded, and escorted Petula onto the podium in the winner's circle like a jockey walking a thoroughbred, then watched as last year's queen hurriedly crowned her. The crowd went ballistic. Petula had the crown back, where it rightfully belonged, on her overbleached, hair-extensioned 'do.

"Oh, but before you go, how about one for the yearbook!" Petula said as she landed a huge kiss on Damen's lips in front of the cameras.

Damen wasn't even angry. The same old Petula was back. She knew instinctively the picture the photogs wanted and she gave it to them. She put her arms around his neck, leaned into him again, and whispered in his ear. He tried to pull away this time, but lingered for a second, surprised at what he heard.

"Thank you," Petula said softly.

It was the most sincere thing she'd ever said to him. He felt forgiven, and even more in a rush than before to get to Scarlet.

As the football players ran out, Petula got back to business, pushing him aside and posing down solo with her crown, making sure the Wendys were stationed just outside the frame. Damen snuck away, practically unnoticed by the throng.

Before he could clear out completely, Josh sauntered up to him and blocked his path.

"Hey, Dylan," he said condescendingly, holding out his hand limp-wristed. "Just wanted to congratulate you."

Damen started to move around him, all the anger he'd been feeling now taking second place to his desire to get back and hold Scarlet. But Josh wouldn't let him by.

"At least your girlfriend knows how to win. Not like your pathetic defense last season."

"Have you ever heard," Damen started slowly, "that the best defense is a good offense."

Damen balled up his right fist and smacked Josh in the mouth, decking him.

"No offense," Damen scoffed for good measure.

He wasn't a violent guy by nature, but beating Josh down, felt, well . . . great.

As he made his way off the field he saw a familiar face racing toward it. It was Kiki. News must have gotten back to her that Petula and her miraculous dress had made it to Homecoming after all.

She was screaming Petula's name and something he couldn't quite make out through the crowd noise and her own obvious tears of joy.

Was it "she's alive," he thought ambivalently, or "it's Alive." Damen laughed to himself as he turned to watch their tender embrace, and decided that, when it came to describing Petula, there wasn't much difference.

The crowd continued to shout its approval long after the announcement.

Petula checked her crown, repositioning it, and at that moment, she remembered some advice that Virginia had given her. She said that the outgoing queens always wanted to sabotage the incoming queen's moment, so they always put the crown on crooked.

She closed her eyes and channeled her little friend, trying with all her heart and, using the term loosely, soul, to share this victory with her.

Her memorial concluded, Petula freed herself of her ankle monitor, which left everyone in the audience thinking that she was now ready to party.

Love and *haterade* was raining down on Petula from every girl in the stands as she took her victory lap, smiling and waving condescendingly as if nothing had ever happened. The Wendys were in awe at the outpouring.

"Do you think it's the coma diet?" Wendy Anderson wondered aloud cattily.

"Maybe," Wendy Thomas said. "Let's try it for prom."

Petula looked back at the Wendys following resentfully in their cars behind her.

It was just as she'd always dreamed it would be.

ॐ

Damen walked in the room and moved toward Scarlet's bed uneasily. She was there, lying still, and to him, this was not a good sign. It was not what he was expecting. As he drew

closer, he could feel her breath on his cheek. It was not as labored as it had been. He moved in even closer and brushed his lips against hers lightly.

"You have lipstick on your mouth!" Scarlet said with her eyes still closed.

Damen, startled out of his mind, jumped away from the bed.

"You couldn't even wait until the body was cold, could you?" Scarlet said, slowly opening her eyes.

"Scarlet!" he said, grabbing her face and kissing her, then backing away to look at her. "Don't ever leave me again."

"Now you know how I feel when you're away at college," she replied with a smirk, still a little groggy.

"I can't believe you found her. Who knew Petula had a soul?"

She laughed and looked up at him, the relief of being with him again shining from her hazel eyes. A solitary tear dropped from Damen's eye.

"Is that a tear?"

"Yeah, but it's a man-tear."

"The next thing you know you'll be wearing guyliner, but that wouldn't be such a bad thing."

Damen held Scarlet's face in his hands. Their smiles wiped from their mouths as they gazed into each other's eyes.

"Did you give Charlotte a kiss from me?" Damen asked, grateful to Charlotte for bringing Scarlet back to him.

"I don't kiss girls," Scarlet replied sarcastically, but knowing just how much Damen's saying that would mean to Charlotte.

"I do," Damen said, giving her a soft kiss.

"What, I risk my life, cross over to the other side, bring my sister back, and that's all I get?"

"Scarlet," Damen said in all sincerity, stroking her porcelain skin on her cheek with his thumb.

"Yeah?"

"I . . . love you," Damen said, punctuating every word.

"And it only took a near-death experience to get that out of you?" Scarlet whispered into his ear while embracing him.

"I love you too," Scarlet said, kissing him as if her life depended on it.

꘠

Charlotte escorted Virginia to Dead Ed, first through the Hawthorne Middle School Virginia attended and then through the familiar halls of the adjacent High School.

"I'm glad I at least got to see it," Virginia said sadly of the bastion of higher learning.

"Yeah, well," Charlotte said sweetly, recalling her years there and putting the best spin on the present situation, "it wasn't all that."

Virginia appreciated Charlotte's sensitivity but could see from the wistful look on her face that she might not have been telling the whole truth.

"You know, when my friend Pam first brought me here, she tried to make me laugh because I was so nervous," Charlotte said, trying her best to comfort Virginia. "She said, look on the bright side, you don't have to shave anymore."

Virginia thought that was kinda funny but then realized she'd never shaved before, and now, she never would. Charlotte was trying so hard that Virginia cracked a little smile for her sake. As they walked down the corridor to the main lobby, Virginia was anxious to change the subject, and saw something that would do just the trick.

"Isn't that you?" Virginia asked, pointing to the Hawthorne Wall of Fame showcase.

"It was," Charlotte said peacefully.

Charlotte stopped for a second, studying her yearbook photo and her obituary, which sat in the center of sports, debate team, Mathlete trophies, and year after year of class and alumni photos, just as Scarlet had told her. Under her headshot it read "Her memory will live in these halls forever."

It had been a long time since she'd seen herself, living or dead, and she thought about how young she looked, even though she'd never look any different. She was grouped with the Noted Alumni, which made her feel proud, even though it might have all been some kind of joke. She couldn't be sure, but it didn't matter to her anymore. She had been remembered after all, and fondly too. The newspaper would yellow soon, she thought, and the

photo would fade, but then, so would everybody else's. She'd been here, been alive, for a while. That was enough for her now.

"Looks like you made quite an impression. Were you a cheerleader or something?" Virginia asked.

"Not exactly," Charlotte said before she paused and changed the subject. "Virginia, some lives are long, some are short, but they're all important and they all must come to an end. This is forever. It's taken me a long time to figure that out."

Virginia wrapped her small hands around Charlotte's neck, squeezing her tightly, and Charlotte knew that she had made an impression too.

"Hey, you have a pretty good grip. Where were you when I was choking on that gummy bear?"

Before Virginia could ask what she was talking about, they both noticed the projector light flooding the hallway from the Dead Ed class at the end of the hallway.

"This is it," Virginia said nervously, grasping Charlotte's hand tightly.

"That's it," Charlotte confirmed, remembering having said the very same thing to herself.

Charlotte walked her, hand in hand, to the doorway, and turned the knob. She peeked in at the darkened classroom, heard the whirr of the projector spindle turning, and saw the silhouettes of the classmates, sitting and waiting. She felt like it was either just yesterday or ages ago that she'd been there.

Charlotte gestured for the girl to enter and Virginia walked in — alone. As the door closed, Charlotte heard the words that let her know Virginia would be okay.

"Welcome, Virginia. We've been expecting you."

Epilogue

This Must Be the Place

I've been to paradise, but I've never been to me
—Charlene

We all want to get to a better place.

———•✦•———

Whether it's getting to a better place in our physical lives: breaking off a damaging relationship or starting a new one, or spiritually finding a better place, a sort of plane to exist on, or the Big Mama of them all—Heaven. Charlotte spent her whole Life, and Afterlife, trying to get to a better place until she finally realized that there wasn't a place to get to— that the better place was actually inside of her the whole time. She was changed now and what she was becoming definitely outweighed what she'd lost.

hatever personal growth Charlotte had experienced on her journey back to Hawthorne, she was still feeling lonely as she trudged uphill through the woods. She was confident that she'd put Damen and Petula, and the dreams of her childhood, behind her for good, but she still felt that same emptiness inside. Maybe it was just her fear of facing Markov that was bugging her. She still had a lot to explain after all. She'd put lives at risk. Lying, leaving the compound, missing work. All of it. Things might have turned out very badly. She could only hope that Pam and Prue had paved the way for her, at least a little.

She gave herself some credit for her accomplishments too, however, which was very unlike her. Everyone was where they belonged now. She had gotten rid of Maddy, and by helping Scarlet help Petula, she'd connected Virginia with her Dead

Ed class. It would just be a matter of time before they crossed over. Given all the work she'd done, maybe she could explain to Markov that she was away on a business trip. But if she had to pay, then so be it.

"Nice to have you back," Mr. Markov said, nodding as Charlotte passed him on the way back to her desk.

"Nice to be back."

It was business as usual, except that Maddy was gone. Her phone had been disconnected, the cord wrapped around it several times for good measure.

Everyone looked busy, and Charlotte walked by glumly with her head down, not ready to look anyone in the eye just yet. When she arrived at her desk, she noticed that Pam and Prue were not taking calls. They were packing.

She was petrified that she was about to be left behind again, the price she had paid for blowing her second chance.

"Usher!" a familiar voice called out. "I want to see you in my office!"

She gathered herself, cleared her throat, and walked slowly toward Markov's office — the source of the Voice.

When she'd finally mustered up the courage, she entered to find a male figure standing next to the window, his back to her. As he turned around, she recognized his face.

"Mr. Brain!"

"Charlotte," Mr. Brain said warmly, just as happy to see her.

"Where have you been? Why are you here?"

"I've been right there," he said sternly, pointing to the tiny

camera that had been hovering over Charlotte in the call center.

"I don't understand."

"I've been watching you the whole time."

Charlotte bowed her head, humiliated. After all she'd said and done, to know that Brain was watching the whole time was too embarrassing to contemplate.

"You were tested," Brain acknowledged, "but you didn't fail."

"I didn't?" Charlotte wondered, totally confused. "But I was so tempted. I almost . . ."

"Remember we once discussed that good or bad outcomes are the result of choices, of actions, not intentions."

"Who did I help with my choices?" Charlotte asked dejectedly. "I didn't even get one lousy phone call."

"Scarlet was your call. She was the one who needed you the most."

"But she almost lost everything because of me. Her sister, her boyfriend, even her life."

"On the contrary, you gave all those things back to her."

"But, I never listened," Charlotte said, making the case against herself. "I did what I wanted, not what I was told to do, what everyone thought I *should* do."

"Exactly," Brain replied.

"I didn't do what *you* told me to do," Charlotte emphasized sheepishly.

"You did what your heart told you to do," Brain complimented. "It is what leaders, not followers, do."

Charlotte still couldn't fully process where Brain was going. It sounded like the Afterlife would be one big psychotherapy session. She was beginning to feel like she needed a mental health day.

"Was the whole point of crossing over just to help others?" Charlotte probed Mr. Brain, frustrated. "What about me?"

"Sometimes a good deed really *is* its own reward, Charlotte. Sometimes that is all there is."

"Whoever called this the final reward must have been on something," Charlotte joked.

"I said *sometimes*, Charlotte. Not always."

Charlotte wasn't really listening any longer. She started toward Brain, to hug him, thank him for not punishing her, and promise that nothing like that would ever happen again.

As she approached him, Mr. Brain motioned for Charlotte to head to the back office.

"Charlotte, you've taken care of everyone else. Now it's time to take care of you."

Charlotte entered the office and saw a couple sitting down.

"They have been waiting to see you for quite a while," Mr. Brain said. "Over fifteen years, to be exact."

"Hello, Angel," the woman said in a hauntingly familiar voice.

The couple stood up expectantly, and Charlotte ran to them. They hugged as if they were trying to squeeze into a single being.

Charlotte's heart, a heart that had been searching for love for so long, came to life. She realized that she had been home-sick for a place she never knew, until now.

"Charlotte," Brain began, "this is your mother and father."

"I know," Charlotte replied.

The end?

Acknowledgments

Thank you to my mother, Beverly, for all of your love and encouragement, and to Oscar Martin, my little blessing.

Special thanks to my fairy godmother, editor extraordinaire Nancy Conescu, for waving your wand and making all of this real.

My heartfelt gratitude for all of those who helped bring ghostgirl to life: Craig Phillips, Megan Tingley, Lawrence Mattis, Andy McNicol, Alison Impey, Vincent Martin, Deborah Bilitski, Mary Nemchik, Tom Hurley, Andrea Spooner, Christine Cuccio, Amy Verardo, Andrew Smith, Tina McIntyre, Lisa Sabater, Lisa Ickowicz, Jonathan Lopes, Melanie Chang, Shawn Foster, Lauren Nemchik, Mary Pagnotta, and Chris Murphy.

ghostgirl author **Tonya Hurley**'s credits span all platforms of teen entertainment, including: creating, writing, and producing two hit TV series, writing and directing several acclaimed independent films, developing a groundbreaking collection of video games and board games, and creating and providing content for award-winning websites. Ms. Hurley lives in New York with her husband and daughter.

Romance is dead in

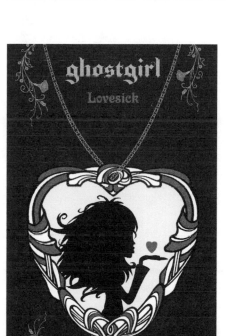

ghostgirl
Lovesick

by Tonya Hurley

the third to-die-for book in the *New York Times* bestselling ghostgirl series

harlotte," a gentle voice called out, "It's time to wake up now."

"Wake up?" Charlotte thought, still groggy and submerged in sleep.

The voice was sweetly familiar, one that she had archived in her memory as well as her heart but that still could only barely penetrate the wall of sleep she'd built around herself. It seemed to come both from everywhere and no place in particular. Charlotte felt it more than she heard it, and she'd been "feeling" it much more often now that she was so prone to oversleeping.

"Come on," the voice pleaded a bit more urgently. "You're going to be late."

As Charlotte came to, she realized that she really hadn't been sleeping so much as resting. Not for the sake of her body—that need had passed along with her life—but for her mind. She was happier than she'd ever been, but also nervous, jittery, and preoccupied, the way you feel whenever a major change approaches.

It was the kind of feeling of both relief and expectation she'd had at the end of every school year. No more pencils, no more books. No more teachers, classmates, hall monitors, lunchroom ladies, bus drivers, or dirty looks. Summer was coming, full of freedom and possibility. The only difference now was that summer could last forever. In fact, she was counting on it.

"Charlotte Usher! Get up this minute!"

Charlotte's eyes flung open as if a ripcord had pulled them. She looked around the room and let out a sigh of relief.

I'm still here, Charlotte thought. *It's all still here.*

It was the same thing every morning. She would hear the voice and then question if it was real or if everything was just some crazy dream. If she were still alive, she might have thought she was becoming demented, but the nice thing about being dead was that she didn't have to worry about losing it. So, scratch that.

Maybe, Charlotte thought, it was just that she'd been filled with longing, even pain, for so long that she wasn't used to being happy. Not that she was one hundred percent elated all the time, though. As wonderful as her reunion with her parents had been, it had come with certain disadvantages. She'd gotten used to being alone and had always prized her autonomy, which was more and more in dispute these days. She was increasingly accountable now, not only to her parents, but also to her intern supervisor, Markov, and the hotline hysterics. It was a lot of change to process.

"Charlotte!" the voice rang out again, this time in a tone that was very, very real.

"I'm up!" she yelled, pulling the drapes back.

The only thing that made waking up easier these days was the knowledge that it would all be over soon—the early mornings, the depressing phone calls, and the responsibility. Today was the last day at the afterlife intern office.

"Charlotte, sweetheart," her mother spoke as she planted herself down on her bed, "Is everything, you know, okay?"

Her mother wanted so much to impart wisdom whenever she could, seeing as she'd missed out on a lifetime of it, but she'd learned not to press too hard. They hadn't had the day-to-day conflicts that plague many mother-daughter relationships, but that didn't change the fact that there was still a warehouse full of emotional baggage that Charlotte had yet to unpack. And more than a carry-on of it was family-related.

Charlotte turned slowly from the window and faced her. "Mom?" she asked, as if she wanted to hear herself say it but still wasn't used to it.

"Yes, monkey puff?" Eileen eagerly replied, with just a trace of worry in her voice. She tried to make up for a lifetime of terms of endearment, which often resulted in mushy mash-ups.

Charlotte took a deep breath and her eyes widened.

"Never mind," she said, and hurriedly headed for the door. "Love you."

"Love you too," Eileen called after, the closing front door clipping her farewell and their conversation.

☯

On the way to the intern office, Charlotte picked up Pam and Prue, just as she did each morning. They were old friends by now, honest with each other to a fault. The no-holds-barred girl talk, which was as eye-opening as a cup of espresso, was always the best part of her day. As they walked, Charlotte filled them in on her morning.

"Don't you feel comfortable enough with her yet to open up about your boyfriend?" Pam asked.

Pam was hoping Charlotte's mom might drum some sense into her about Eric, the new boy she'd been "dating."

"Did she try to have 'the talk'?" Prue asked, bursting into laughter.

Charlotte felt bad about the fact that she had never gotten "the talk" or even had a reason for it until now.

"I just didn't feel like discussing my love life with my mother, that's all," Charlotte said as they made their way to the phone bank once more. "It's just weird."

"Is it because he's older?" Prue teased.

"He's not really older," Charlotte said. "We're almost the same age; he's just been dead longer."

"Oh, well, that explains it," Prue sneered sarcastically.

The fact that he'd been dead longer was actually a big part

of his appeal to Charlotte. She'd always thought of herself as an old soul, even when she was alive, and there was a realness about Eric that she found missing in most guys she'd known, Damen excluded, of course. Eric was a throwback to another time, not very long ago, in fact; and that, to her, was not a bad thing.

"Have you kissed him?" Pam asked, wanting to hear some juicy, revealing details.

"Don't encourage this, Pam," Prue jumped in. "You know she can't have a *real* kiss with him."

"Maybe not a *living* kiss," Charlotte replied defensively, "but we can still be close."

Yet another downside of being dead, Charlotte thought.

"Do you love him?" Pam asked, poking around to see how far gone Charlotte was.

"Yeah, I think I do," Charlotte admitted out loud for the first time.

"But Charlotte," Pam chided. "You barely know him."

What Pam actually meant to say, Charlotte thought, *was* we *barely know him.* She was just being protective, as a good friend should be. The fact that Eric had transferred in after they'd arrived, pretty much taking that sneaky saboteur Maddy's open seat, made the other interns a little suspicious, no matter how nice he seemed. That he had been a musician in life didn't exactly score him a lot of brownie points with Pam and Prue either.

"Never mind him," Prue said, skeptically. "What do you know about *love?*"

It was a fair question, but not one that Pam or Prue could answer either, and Charlotte knew it. Not that it stopped them from badgering her.

"I don't *know* anything about it," Charlotte shot back. "But I know what I *feel*."

"Well, *I* feel like we've been down this road before," Prue barked, her disapproval showing.

"What is that supposed to mean?" Charlotte quizzed indignantly.

"It means you're carrying on just like you did with Damen," Pam said. "You're obsessed. Again."

"Look where that got you," Prue reminded. "And this guy is no Damen."

Charlotte held her tongue and thought for a second about what the girls were trying to tell her. It was true; Eric was nothing like Damen on the outside. Actually, he was almost the exact opposite. The way he dressed, his lifestyle, his ambitions. Not the kind of guy Charlotte would ever have considered as a soul mate.

She'd gotten to know him though — the real him, she liked to say. And underneath the leather, chains, and spiky hairdo, Eric was sweet and kind. He was also monopolizing more and more of her free time, which is what Charlotte thought this whole chat was really about anyway.

"I think you're both jealous," Charlotte fired back. "That I finally found someone."

"Don't be so defensive," Pam said. "We're just looking out for you."

"I'm not being defensive," Charlotte complained. "But here I am telling you how happy I finally am and you're both lecturing me like I'm a child."

"Maybe that's because you still haven't learned your lesson," Pam chided.

"Which is?" Charlotte pressed.

"Love is for the living," Pam answered. "It's one of the first discussions we ever had, remember?"

"You said that's why they call it a love *life*," Charlotte recalled. "I remember."

"You've made so much progress," Pam said sweetly, "and now you're jeopardizing it for a guy you just met."

Everyone took a breath to reload. Pam and Prue knew Charlotte well enough to know that she was nowhere near ready to concede.